'What you gunna do?' he says

Then I tell him. I'm going to have the baby.

'And anyway,' I say. 'Don't you mean – what're *we* gunna do? It's *your* baby too.'

He's slumped there, motionless, except for when he swigs from his can of fizzy orange. Doesn't answer for a minute. Then, 'How do I know it's mine? he says.

Y'see, Liam can make me feel good, like no one else can. Or Liam can make me feel like dirt.

from The Women's Press

Sandra Chick is the author of *Push Me, Pull Me* (Livewire, 1987), winner of The Other Award for progressive Children's Literature; a Feminist Book Fortnight 'Selected Twenty' title; and shortlisted for the *Observer* Teenage Fiction Prize 1987. She has also written *I Never Told Her I Loved Her* (Livewire, 1989), *On the Rocks* (Livewire, 1996), and *Cheap Street* (Livewire, 1998). She has two daughters.

Don't Look
Back

Sandra Chick

First published by Livewire Books, The Women's Press Ltd, 1999
A member of the Namara Group
34 Great Sutton Street, London EC1V 0LQ

Copyright © Sandra Chick 1999

The right of Sandra Chick to be identified as the author of this work has
been asserted by her in accordance with the Copyright, Designs and
Patents Act 1988.

British Library Cataloguing-in-Publication Data
A catalogue record for this book is available from the British Library.

This book is sold subject to the condition that it shall not, by way of trade
or otherwise, be lent, re-sold, hired out, or otherwise circulated without
the Publisher's prior consent in any form of binding or cover other than
that in which it is published and without a similar condition including
this condition being imposed on the subsequent purchaser.

ISBN 0 7043 4958 2

Typeset in 12/14pt Bembo by FSH Ltd, London
Printed and bound in Great Britain by Cox & Wyman Ltd, Reading,
Berkshire

Part One

One

I don't know anything about kids. Weird, they are. Like, in a nano second they can transform themselves from fluffy-wuffy bunnies into psycho turds; thugs from playtown. Zac can, anyway. No warning, no nothing. And I don't suppose he's any different from the rest. Does it all the time. And there's nothing cutesy about a three-year-old, laying fists and feet into his mother for all he's worth. It's just not funny. It's *grim*, in fact.

Poor old Mel. Everyone says that – *poor old Mel* – as if that's her name in full. Not that she is old – poor maybe, I'll give you that – but not yet twenty. Looks younger, on the outside; but has to be older, on the inside.

'Come on,' she says, quietly, firmly. 'Calm down and tell me what's up, little man.'

I hate that – *little man*. Little git, more like. Little pain in the rear end.

He's pointing to the seat of his trousers, now. Ugh . . .

But Mel can hack it, the whole scene. Keep her cool, keep her chin up. If it was me I'd . . . I don't know what I'd do. But then, like I said, I don't know anything about it. At the minute, I feel like I don't know anything about anything.

Mel — she's my best mate Sarah's sister — was just hitting seventeen when she had Zac. Old enough. I mean, it's not illegal, is it? But young at the same time. Just a bit older than I am, now. So I wonder — how come she knows how to handle it, and I don't? Is there such a thing as a 'natural', or did she have to learn?

I've never even held a baby, not properly. Not for longer than I've had to. And then only because everyone thinks you'll be offended if they don't let you. Offering their squashy, damp bundle like it's an armful of tenners or something.

'Here . . .' they say. 'Want a cuddle?' Giving you no choice in the matter, whatsoever. After all, you can hardly look up and say, 'No thanks. I'd rather have me nails torn out with pliers and made into a pair of exotic earrings,' can you?

Babies scare me. They're too soft and floppy and delicate for my liking. All gurgly, sicky and . . . I don't even want to think about it. I've never been one to go gooey like some people do; a puppy, a kitten, a kid. They've never made me flutter and flatter like some dimwit. More like — shut down and yawn. Not that I'd want them to come to harm; it's just I've never been interested.

But, right now, I can't think about anything else.

I mean, p'raps I'm panicking, before time. I could just be

4

late… P'raps it'll be all right, a false alarm. 'Cause it wasn't meant to be like this.

If I am all right, I'll never risk it again – and that's a promise. I just didn't think it'd happen – not to me. I don't know why. I just thought… Oh, I don't know what I thought.

But I'm pretty sure it has happened. I *know* it's happened. I'm pregnant. *Up the duff. In the club. One in the oven.* And I'm scared. Dead scared. Not ready for all this …

I can't tell anyone. Can't get me head around it. And if I tell someone, it'll make it real. Definite. Everything'll start rolling and I won't be able to stop it. Stop *them*. Lecturing me, talking down to me, telling me this, telling me that. Like, all of them making out they're perfect – they've never made a mistake in their lives. They'll not even try to understand. Just go on about how stupid I am. How I should've known better. They'll all have *opinions* and maybe they'll be right, but I'm not ready. Not yet.

'That's it, Zac. That's better,' Mel says, slowly. In complete control over the muddied wet wipes. 'Now get yourself a biscuit and a clean pair of pants.' *Charming.* She's wafting the rancid smell away with her hand. 'Not to worry,' she says as he scurries off towards the kitchen; clean bummed, but still sticky faced with a hollering gob on him, shouting clap trap.

'He's really… lively,' I say, feeling awkward, searching for a compliment of sorts.

'Yeh,' she says. 'I'm really proud of him, y'know. He's a good boy – most of the time, anyway. Gets a bit demanding, sometimes. Gets bored easy… needs stimulating.'

So that's what it is? And I thought he was just a stinking little toe-rag with a snot factory in the middle of his mush and a loose bowel somewhere down below.

There's a crash in the kitchen.

'What now?' she calls, jumping up to investigate the clunk and clatter that follows. Not that he could ruin anything in this hole; everything's already worn out and past it. Second rate, third hand luxuries; I mean – the stretch nylon covered settee – all flowers and fag burns. The collection of cheap, chalky ornaments – a dazzling variety of juggling clowns. And as for the fuzzy loo seat cover – you wouldn't want t' park your back end on *there*, that's for sure.

Zac's playing the innocent with her.

'Not my fault,' I hear him whine. 'It weren't me.'

'Oh, Zac...' sharper this time, more like normal mothers do. Though not as sharp as my mother used to be – and there's no slapped, stinging legs neither.

I know Mum – and she's gunna kill me – when she finds out. And I really mean *she's gunna kill me*.

Smug, she is. Dead smug. She'll demand all the gory details – like, why and when? As if it matters, makes any difference. As if she's the bleeding Virgin Mary or somethin' – when, in reality, she's got *nothin'* t' shout about. But it won't stop her. I know she can't talk – but she will. She'll talk and talk. For the rest of her life, she'll talk. She'll *die* talking at me. And I can't bear the thought. The sound, the noise, the fuss and commotion. The instructions and the sneering. Not yet. Not ever.

I don't care what she thinks, anyway. I only care about Liam. What he thinks. I only care about not losing him and about...oh, I don't know how I feel. Confused. Boxed in; that's how I feel. I feel like running. Like I'm being chased. Being suffocated. But there's no way out. Can't blag me way out've *this*. I'm not clever and canny any more – and just being lippy means nothing now.

Plenty people must risk it...But it has to be me that gets caught. It has to be me that gets it all wrong and messes up. So p'raps they'll all have the right t' call me stupid. But it doesn't give them the right t' push me around, does it? And even though I feel like I might cave in, I mustn't let them see it, or I'll just be dirt under their feet. Though I can't shake off this feeling – that I'm being...swallowed up. I'm being swallowed up and I'm scared.

Zac hugs Mel's legs as she tries to walk back into the front room. She's gotten rid of the stinky pants and is drying her reddened hands with a grubby, checked tea towel.

'Go and play,' she says to him. '*Nicely*.'

'You didn't say *please*,' he says, smart arse fashion.

'*Please*,' she says quietly, wiping around her fistful of silvery rings. Looking towards me and putting on a voice, 'I can't stand faeces in me diamonds, can you?' Smiling, twisting the stainless steel bands. I smile back because I'm supposed to.

Her mum's flat still whiffs.

'Does he do that a lot?' I say.

She laughs.

'Your face!' Then, 'No. Well. Now and again he'll have the odd accident.'

Puts a tape in the cassette player and starts to tidy about, half dancing. Looking cool; 'with it', as me gran would've put it.

Mel's a proper funky mother. Not like mine – who just thinks she is. Makes me die with every tottering, skin-tight step. She's definitely 'without it', but doesn't realise. She says she likes to 'make the effort'. Seems to think she's glam and kittenish – right down to her fake tan and knitted hair-do – all permed and prancing.

Dan the Man (*her* man), loves it, it seems. Right up his street. Said to me once – that it's a pity I'm not more like her – meaning in looks and ways.

'You're chalk and cheese,' he said, the fat prat thinking he was wounding me deeply.

Huh. Crack open a bottle, I say – p'raps life's not such a bummer after all.

I'm more like me dad, they say. Which I wouldn't know – on account he's kept his head down and his money in his pocket for the best part of sixteen years. He did come to see me a couple of times, but not so often that I remember his face. It was a long time ago. I used to have a blurry photo of him – but I binned it one day, in temper.

'How's Liam?' Mel asks.

'All right.'

'You living at his mum's still?'

'Yeh.'

'Sarah said you were stopping there. Is it okay?'

'Yeh. S'all right. Till we find somewhere – a flat . . .'

'That's good,' she says. 'Lookin' around, are you?'

'Looking . . .' I say.

'That's what I'd like – me own flat,' she says. 'Get out from under me mum's feet . . . Much about?'

'Not much . . .'

8

I don't let on – that it's not good. Not even *all right*. It's crap – Liam's the only good thing. Special, he is.

Liam wanted me when no one else did. Gran was poorly; and *Mum* didn't want me – not since the day *Dan* walked into her life.

Sarah still hasn't shown up. But then, I only called in on the off-chance...

I sit there for a bit longer, trying to think of something else to say. Mumbling something now and again. Out of embarrassment as much as anything; feeling awkward. Trying to be friendly.

Trying to forget. Failing.

I ought to take a test. Go to the doctor. But it's like I'm waiting – as if – if I wait long enough – it's going to get sorted out, on its own. Resolve itself and everything'll be okay. And like I said – I'll never chance it again... *Please* God, make it okay... *and I'll never chance it again*, I swear.

Even though I know it's too late, I'm still kidding meself.

Mel starts reading the paper. Wittering on... rubbish. Girl power hype. Well, mine's washed up – shot to bits right now – and I don't want to know. I don't feel powerful; I feel drained.

I *can't* have a baby. I can't *not* have it, either.

'You all right?' she asks.

'Yeh,' I say. 'Okay.'

'Don't seem yourself...'

'I'm okay.'

The silences are getting dead uncomfortable. I'm worried she's sussed me. Will start asking questions I don't want to hear and can't answer. Like I might blurt it all out or something – and that's the last thing I need; I need a full confessional, like I need a punch in the chops.

It's got to be time to go. I stand up.

'I'll catch Sarah later, maybe...' shrugging. 'Got some things t' do.'

'You sure? You're welcome to hang around...'

'No, s'all right.' Then, 'Don't get up,' I say, 'I'll see meself out.'

But she comes to the door, anyhow.

'Don't know where she's got to... I'll tell her you came round.'

'If you like,' I say. 'No big deal... I'll catch up with her, sometime.'

I forget to say thanks for the tea. That'd have me gran hopping; she was always big on manners.

'Didn't they teach you *anythin'* at school?' she'd say. No, actually. Not a lot. Didn't exactly break me heart to leave.

Wasn't brilliant tea, anyway. Too much milk and only as warm as a smacked arse. Gran wouldn't have approved of that either – it'd have to be steaming hot and orangey brown. Enough to take the skin off your lips and blister the roof of your mouth.

I haven't seen me gran in a while. Feel bad. But I just *can't*.

It was always her thing – y'know – that she'd be dumped in some home and never see anyone, this month to next. No visitors, no nothing. And that's what it might look like; but it's not really like that.

She doesn't know what day it is any more.

I'm not even sure what a stroke actually means – besides being a fancy medical name for cruelty. Indignity. Torture.

They say – she's got *this* wrong – she's got *that* wrong – when all I want is to have the old gran back. Spirited and in charge. The bittersweet Gran who'd rip your face off at forty paces – but be there when you needed her.

They said, she might improve, with time. But now they don't say anything much and I can't bear it. Can't bear to see her crumpled, spent and half mad. Frustrated and kiddish; talking dross. It's been hard. Really hard. She knew a lot of things, me gran. And now she's lost.

Sarah's mum's, to home, isn't that far so I walk. To *Liam's mum's* I mean – not really what I'd call *home*. But like I said, it's just for now, just temporary. I had to move out of Gran's, where I used to live – and you can forget Mum and Dan's – I wish Dan'd drop down dead. But we haven't been able to find a place on our own yet. Not one we can afford. So. We're still with Evelyn. Or *Eve* as she aspires to be known – trying to French herself up a bit – trying to be something she's not, again. All this swank, when really she's as jagged as hell. Gets right up my nose.

'*Course you could get a job – if you wanted one*.' Like, has *she* tried? Obviously not – but *I* have. Then it's, 'Don't mooch about – *do* something. And turn that blasted noise down!'

Ratty cow. Like everything's got t' be perfect and peaceful all the time.

I wish she'd drown in her sea of man-made fibres, get strangled by her yards of creamy net. I mean – two coats of magnolia emulsion and she reckons we're living in a palace? Well, we're not; all told, it's a grotty maisonette, on the edge of a grotty estate in an equally grotty town. It's cruddy, drab and full of tat.

11

God knows what *she'll* have to say about me. Doubtless it'll be forthcoming and plenty. Spurting and spouting just like the rest. She doesn't even like me and Liam sharing a room. I'm not good enough – not what she had in mind, or hoped for – but she doesn't want to upset her precious boy by saying it outright.

She's on me, as soon as I get inside. Calls out.

'Lisa, is that you? Hang your jacket on the peg and *don't slam the door like that.* You'll break the glass.' Her raspy voice grating me ear holes.

She's sat at the table, telly on.

'All right?' I say.

'All right,' tan-tipped fag in one hand, a glass of something yellowy in the other. The parting of her thin plummy bob hits me in the eye, is blindingly mauve again from cheap dye.

'Liam back?'

'Shhh,' she goes. 'I'm watching this.' Sucks her cigarette. Smoke billowing out of her flaring nostrils. Then. 'Haven't seen hide nor hair of 'im. What time's he meant to be home?' Completely disinterested.

I just shrug.

I mean – as if *I'd* know.

He never says when he'll be home. Early, late, whatever... Gets narked if I 'keep on', so I try not to ask. Don't want to start anything.

He's been dead tetchy lately. Says he doesn't need it – me, going on at him – not when he's been out at work all day.

He's only been in the job a few weeks. Labouring. 'Digging holes and shifting shite', as he puts it. He says he still has to prove himself yet – they won't keep him on if he's a clock-watcher or a skiver. Or if he doesn't fit in with the rest of the lads. And I know it's the only way we'll get a place to ourselves, so I'm careful with him. But it would be nice to know. Where he's been, who with and all that; what's going on, any news. They all go out, down the pub when they've finished, see, for a chat and a lark; boys only. And a drink, course.

Mind you, we've had some right times this past few months, since we've been together.

Some brilliant times. Proper fun, daft and dangerous. Messing about, doing what we felt like; doing what we damn well wanted.

Belonging. That's been the best bit, *belonging*. And for the first time, I've *liked being me*.

One night, right, we got hold of this push bike. We're riding along, me on the handlebars, through the estate, when we pass this house with the front door wide open. Liam only jumps off and legs it inside – comes out beaming – with a picture from off the wall! Shoves it on top of me and pedals for all we're worth. Can't see a thing – and going like the clappers, we are. All the way down Solomon Drive and out the other side. Did we have a laugh?! Like, imagine this poor old geezer – looking up to find a picture's been nicked off his wall while he was casually making a cup of tea in the next room or somethin'!

We felt tight after, mind – kept meaning t' take it back – leave it in the front garden or somewhere. But then Evelyn saw it, caught us on the hop and Liam told her we'd bought it for her down the boot sale, as a surprise.

'For me?' she goes, glowing. 'I don't know what t' say.' Dead touched, she was. Hung it over the gas fire, pride of place and all. Bloody horrible it is, too. A golden eagle against the setting sun. Ugly as hell. But every time I look at it, I smile. I'll nudge Liam sometimes – or catch his eye – and we'll giggle about it. She gets narked 'cause she doesn't know what we're on about – thinks we're taking the mick out've her. Which we are, in a way.

Another time, was when we barricaded Liam's mate, Pete, in the gents behind Woolworths. Just left him there...

And when someone got hold of this Bacardi and we all ended up scaling the top of the fir trees down the park...

And when one of the gang planted a dope plant in the police station garden. Just crept in, like...

'You stopping?' Evelyn says. ''Cause if you are, for God's sake sit down. Look like you're waiting for a bus, or somethin'.'

I perch on the edge of the chair for a minute – then slope off upstairs, out of her way.

In a bit, I hear the door go. It's him. Liam.

He calls out to no one in particular.

'Kettle on...?' Gets no response. Comes scuffing up to our room.

'All right?'

'Shot,' he says.

'Hard work?'

'What d'you think?' Crashing down on to the bed.

He looks dirty and gorgeous. Needs to shave. His white tee shirt is covered in muck and the knee is gone from his jeans; split.

He pushes his fingers through his dusty hair, closes his eyes for a minute. Then.

'Come here,' he says, and I move close beside him – messing up the bed as me feet drag the covers.

'What've you been up to all day, then?' he asks.

'Nothing much. Had a cuppa with the Prime Minister...A quick gossip with Her Majesty...The usual.'

'All right for some,' pulling himself up to face me.

I don't like him looking at me. Not close up. I wonder what he sees, when he looks at me like that. The dim and ugly kid that the others see? Or something else, something better and something worth it.

He's never said how he feels – about me, I mean. Doesn't like talking feelings. Or futures, anything like that. *Fun* – he'll talk about that – how we're gunna have the *best* fun. But if I try and get serious, he'll just laugh it off.

'Doom,' he'll grin. 'We're all *doomed*!'

He baffles me sometimes, Liam does. He can make me feel warm with just a look, if he wants to. But he can make me feel cold, too.

I know I've got to tell him but I don't know how. How to say – that it won't make any difference – that we'll still have fun and we'll still...

'Steak and kidney pie...' Evelyn hollers. 'S'ready. Getting cold.'

He sighs, mocking her, '*Steak and kidney pie...*' Smirking. I like it when he takes the rise out of her. Makes me feel like he's more mine than hers, despite what she seems t' think.

'I hate steak and kidney,' I say. 'Let's stay here.'

'You're joking,' he says, hauling himself up. 'I feel half starved.'

I feel sick. Just the thought of food, really turns me up right now.

'Tell her I don't want any. Not hungry.'

'You tell her,' he says. 'She won't bite.'

But she will and she does.

'Not hungry? Why? What's the matter with you, then?' Fast getting snooty. 'Is it not t' your *liking*, madam?' And then harping on, 'You know I hate *waste*, and I've heated it now – won't keep. You youngsters don't seem to realise – you have to *buy* food – it costs *money*.'

'I'll have hers,' Liam says.

'Pig,' she says. 'We'll share it.'

The pong of all that mashed up pie and pastry and peas – it's just too much for me. I make a dash for the downstairs loo.

'What *is* that girl's problem?' I hear her say. 'I've upset her now, I s'pose, have I? Talk about having to take your words out and look at 'em before you speak...', knife and fork scraping the plate, enough to make you shiver.

Liam doesn't answer. Not that I can hear, anyway. No. You can bet on it – he doesn't answer. Lets her get away with it as usual.

I'm good at throwing up quietly. Some people make loads of noise – heaving away, but not me. Quiet and clean, me. Sometimes I think it's the *only* thing I'm any good at – that, and being chicken. Ugh... the very thought of *chicken*.

I wipe me mouth, wipe the bowl with the rough pink paper. Pull the chain and unbolt the door. Make meself scarce. And she can think what she damn well wants.

It really gets to me, though, being shut away in our room most of the time. Feels like a cage; small and cramped. Unless Liam's with me. Then it's all right. Being with him makes everything all right.

Sometimes, when he's out, I get his leather jacket down from the back of the door, breathe in the smell. His smell. Bury me face right in it, I do. And then I look at all his things – his records and posters and tapes. I look at his photo and I'm glad that it's me that's here – not some other girl.

Though other times – lately, it just doesn't work the same. Isn't enough. And I feel trapped, resentful. Hacked off. Thinking – is this it? Is this all there is for me? Stuck in this little room, waiting for me life to start; waiting for him to show up. It's like, he's moving on, on his own – what with getting a job and that. And I have to like it or ditch it.

He soon comes up.

'In a funny mood, aren't you?' he says, matter of fact.

'I'm all right.'

Then, 'Banana and custard,' he says. 'Good grub. You missed out, there,' patting his hard, flat tum.

'Shut up,' I say. 'I don't wanna know.'

He gives me a look.

'Sorry I spoke.' Then, 'What's got into you, anyway?'

Switches the portable on, the picture fuzzy but ready for *Star Trek*. Bends the aerial back and forth but makes it no better. Crashes on to the bed beside me, piling the flat foam pillows behind his neck. Ignoring me.

I wish I felt . . . safer.

I wish he cared a bit more.

Two

Sarah's full of herself. Round at Evelyn's, killing time like usual and she's really got it about her. In line to conquer the universe or some such wild fantasy.

'Grape picking,' she says. 'That's what I'm gunna do – next summer – definite.' Barely pausing, 'You up for it, or what?' I just shrug. 'France,' she says. 'Just imagine it... *France*. It's dead easy work and you get paid loads of money – *and wine* – someone said, last night. Where were you, last night?'

'We stopped in.'

'No. I mean early on – Liam was out... *He's* into it – said so. Didn't he tell you about it?'

I didn't even know he'd seen that lot.

'Liam? He can't go. He's only just found work...'

'Hark at you! You sound like an old married woman! Sound like our Kay...!' Kay's her eldest sister – who's boring and sensible and settled down with a family. Then, 'He's not gunna spend his life fetching and carrying and breaking his back for a few measly quid, is he? I mean, it's not exactly a *brilliant* job, is it? He said as much himself...'

'Did he? What did he say, then? Seems happy enough.'

'Nah. S'all right for now, but he won't stick at it, will he? Can't see him doin' it *forever*, can you? I mean, I know it's money, but...'

'How will *you* afford it, then – getting to France and all that? It costs.'

'It's not a lot. Hardly anything on the ferry – and we can hitch. And – I'm helping out at me mum's place, anyway – soon. Or I might be. In the works canteen. Mornings.'

'What d'*you* know about cooking?!'

'Might not be *cooking*,' she says. 'More than likely be cleaning. Washing up and that.'

'Great.'

'Well, at least it'll get me where I want t' be. Away from this dump. I mean, you're sick of it here, too, aren't you?'

'S'all right. Not bothered.'

'Since when?'

'Well, we've all got *dreams*,' I say. 'But a lot could happen between now and the summer.'

'Yeh,' she says. 'Like what? A whole lot of nothin'.'

She's huffy for a bit. Staring out of the window. Then she turns back, sighing.

'Come on,' she says. 'Say you'll come. A gang of us... Be a laugh.'

'I'll think about it,' I say, to shut her up.

'You do that,' she says, triumphant, grinning her head

off and dancing on the spot with excitement. Anybody'd think she'd just discovered a cure for cancer, or something.

She drops it and starts telling me this grisly story – about how a copper propositioned her mother the other night while he was 'deciding what to do' about a dodgy hi-fi that was sitting nicely in the corner of their front room.

'She told him – take me in and charge me – or get the hell out,' she says, dead proud. 'But it upset her, though. It really did.' Then, about how she got felt up herself, yesterday; getting tea down the chippy.

'Dirty old sod,' she says. Putting on a voice. '"A cod for a cuddle?", he said. "Do that again," I shout, "...and you'll get me fist down your throat."'

She looks to the floor and I doubt she did say that. It's just what she wishes she had the guts to say. Sarah's not a hard case, not really. None of us are, not really. It's all a front – to avoid getting trodden down and worn away.

'How's the old bag?' she asks, changing the subject.

'Keep your voice down,' I say. 'She'll hear.'

'What if she does?'

I shrug.

'It's only for a while,' I say. 'We'll get somewhere, soon.'

She raises her eyebrows, with a 'fat chance' look on her gob, which really irritates me. Still.

'I came over the other day,' I say. 'Did Mel tell you?'

'Nah – she never said. Mind you, I haven't really seen her. I 'spect she's stuck in a mound of washing somewhere. Trying to fight her way through the dribbly vests and holey tights.'

'Zac was a git.'

'Zac's always a git. He's a professional. There's no way I'll ever have a kid after watching Mel struggle . . . It's put me right off.'

'I think she does really well.'

'I'm not knocking her. But she's knackered – and stuck with it. I want a *life*.'

'She really loves him.'

'I know. It's not his fault. I'm just saying – if I ever got caught out . . .'

'What?' I say.

'Well – I'd get rid of it.'

'It's not that simple though, is it?'

'What d'you mean?' she says. '*It is*.'

But I've been looking at this book – only a kid's encyclopedia that Gran gave me, years ago. But it's got a page about pregnancy in it.

At five weeks the baby is already half an inch long. It has a head, a back and a heart. Its mouth and eyes are forming. At eight weeks the baby is one inch long – all the main parts of its body have formed – it even has fingers and toes. And at twelve weeks it has nails and eyelids. It's *five inches long*. How *can I* get rid of it?

We go for a wander, in town.

Sarah looks at clothes and jewellery but can't afford any. I look at shoes and make-up but can't afford any.

It's cold – Sarah wants to go home and get a jacket before coming back to hang around. We split up on the junction where Tindalls Lane meets The Crossway.

'See you later?' she asks.

'Maybe.'

'Go on Lisa – come out tonight.'

21

'Might do . . .' But I think she knows I probably won't.
'What's up?' she says.

'Nothing,' I say. 'I'll see you later.'

I don't feel like going back to Evelyn's; I doubt Liam'll be home. I head for nowhere, traipsing back to the centre, the precinct, the warm.

And as I sit there, huddled up, practically every woman I set eyes on looks fit to deliver a sprog at any minute. Big, stretched, puffy, bulbous women.

I can imagine them, working in banks and offices. Wearing sensible skirts and sensible shoes – and going home to sensible, po-faced husbands who watch rugby and play golf. Have big pay cheques and big ideas.

Proper women, not girls. Nothing like me. They're older and sorted and . . . they've all got this look about them. Almost like – they're waiting for a round of applause or something, because they're somehow . . . *worthy*. Whereas, someone like me – I'm not.

Later on, I follow them around BabyCare. Through the racks of itsy-bitsy velveteen and velour. The blues and oranges, limes and pinks. The prams and pushchairs in tartans and checks, past the shelves stuffed with squidgy soft toys, twenty quid a throw. Boxes of equipment, used for I don't know what. A glut of breastpumps in the sale. Paper pads and bras that flip open and zip up – as nifty as me gran's handbag and just as roomy.

'Can I help at all, dear?' barks some hard-lipped starchy piece in a pencil skirt and a satiny blouse.

'No, thanks . . .' And I turn and go, sharpish.

Leave them to it – poring over, in, around it all. Soaking it up with their credit cards. And I feel second-rate and angry. Like trashing the place. Like giving up.

It's freezing outside, now. Coat pulled round tight, I wish I had some gloves – and I don't mean the ones me gran knitted me last year, a canary yellow nightmare. Shove both hands deep into me pockets and walk fast, as if I've got to be somewhere, soon.

March meself down through the park. Past the little 'uns being pushed to and fro on the swings by icy-faced mums, and the occasional pissed-off dad. Older kids, shivering, shouting and smoking. Standing close, in groups. Under the shelter. Behind the loos. There's a bit of laughter and chasing about. Football. Litter. And enough dog mess to blind thousands. I hate dogs. They slobber and shit far too much.

I know where I'm going but I don't know why.

I go down past the tyre place and the builder's yard. Through the lane, out the other side.

Gran can't help me, not any more. But I just want to walk down this way.

It's a big, old place on the corner – the home. Nothing *homely* about it. Like, if it was done up – it'd be amazing. But it's not and it won't be. Nobody with enough dosh'd want to live down this way. It's hard and cold and a dump.

I stop short of going inside. Stand on the opposite side of the road. Looking. Sit meself down on the wall. Thinking.

I bet it's tea-time about now and she'll be trying to eat and she can't eat properly. And she'll be trying to talk and she can't talk properly. In a minute she'll get nasty, start swearing, accusing, blaming. I want to go in, but I just can't.

It's not so nippy just here, no breeze. I stay and watch

23

for ages. People walking past. A face at the window. A nurse at the door. A car reversing out and driving off; a red Mini, like me uncle Joey used to have.

I wonder what Gran *would've* said, if everything had stayed as it was – as I thought it always would be. If she was still all right, or if she'd suddenly got better, was normal again, overnight.

There's no denying it – she'd lose her rag with me; go berserk, in fact. She'd rant and rave, cuss and curse like a good 'un. Call me soft and Liam worse. Shout about ruined lives and how there was no need for it. She'd come out with all her usual old sayings, 'You'll make your bed, and you'll lie on it', and she'd seethe. 'Little fool!'

Then, in a bit, she'd stop. Calm down. Know she'd said her bit, and that it was my turn.

'Well,' she'd go. 'What're you gunna do about it?'

She'd ask me if I'd really thought it through. *Really* thought it through?

'Forget the smiling baby in the pretty rompers and the bonnets,' she'd say. 'Think about the *reality* for a minute. You've got t' get it straight in your mind – what it is you want.'

She wouldn't take any 'ideal world' crap, neither. She'd be straight down to the facts, straight down the line, straight in your face.

She'd say, 'Do you want it? You don't have t' have it . . .'

She'd talk about nappies and crying, no sleep, no money. She'd talk about responsibilities. The future. She'd say, '. . . and is it fair – on the baby – on the child? 'Cause they don't stay babies for long y'know.'

She'd say I'm not much past a kid meself . . . that 'it seems like only yesterday . . .'

Then she'd start on Liam.

'What's *he* gunna say? Will he stand by you? Or will he do a flit? Think about it,' she'd say. 'Think about all I've said.' Then she'd say again, 'You don't have to have it. But if you decide you want it . . .' Nod and shrug her shoulders. 'I'm sure we'll manage. We'll cope, somehow.'

We, she'd say. It wouldn't just be me; she'd be there, alongside me.

She'd give me some time. Leave me alone.

Put the kettle on, make some tea.

And later, she'd say, 'I'll tell your mother, if you don't want to. Won't be s'many fireworks, that way,' and follow it with one of her winks.

She'd give me the gob but she'd give me a chance. She'd give me the courage.

But Gran's not going to get better.

Not even *she* can fight her way past this, pull herself out. She's tangled up, and like I said before – lost.

Gran was always fierce – but at least she was honest. And she would've understood. One day I'd like to think she would've been proud of me. For having the guts to do what *I* think is right.

Three

Last time I went round to Mum's, she was on about moving. Doesn't like the house they're in, because Dan's ex used to live there with him.

'I can't settle. It's like her... *mark* is stamped on this place. All over,' she said.

Dan muttered something about there being nothing wrong with it. Said Mum's paranoid. Neurotic.

'But for me...?' she droned.

'*Get off my case,*' he said. She was scowling good and proper by the time I left.

When I get round there this time, she's redecorating the kitchen.

'A compromise... of sorts.'

Just started by the looks of it. By herself; Dan's nowhere to be seen. Papering to the strains of Rod Stewart, *Do ya think I'm sexy?* Thinning the paste down to make it go further. Slapping it on – the makeshift table threatening to collapse; an old sheet of formica balanced on two cardboard boxes.

'What d'you reckon?' she asks, holding up a length of soggy 'Country Flowers'. 'Should do the trick?'

'S'all right. If you like that sort of thing.'

'*Smashin*', I thought,' she says, unfazed. 'In the sale as well. Dan wouldn't get it, said it was poncy – and I thought, sod 'im. Went back and got it meself, used this week's food money. He's none the wiser yet. But he will be, when he comes in and finds it like Kew Gardens and there's no tea to boot . . . Serve 'im right. Tight arse.'

'Won't he go mad?'

'Yeh,' she says, dead cool, like. 'Probably.'

Not so long ago, she never would've done that. Or said a word against him – and definitely not to me. But something's changed. It's like she still wants him, wants to be with him; is really jealous and all that. But she's having more of a say, now. Is less wary.

Me uncle Joey's always said she's cynical. A 'cynical bitch', to be precise.

'Knows what she's doing. Plans every move. I should know – I'm her brother – we grew up together.'

She says – brother he may be. Friend he's not.

The thing is, she was putting on an act before. So scared of losing Dan. But you can't put on an act forever. And now she's more how she used to be, before they met. More her old self.

Mind you, *I* still wouldn't be allowed to criticise him. Not even if he was as guilty as hell.

And she still gets on my nerves. Still embarrasses me. Utterly.

Still comes out with things like, '*Now just you listen t' me, young lady,*' jabbing her finger at me, if I so much as breathe out of time. Or, 'Just you behave, or I'll tan your backside' – that's another of her favourites.

She still wears Lycra and is still on a diet. Still thinks that bean bags, grannie boots and Phil Collins records are fashionable and desirable.

'You gunna stand there, gawping, or you gunna help? Get your hands dirty?'

'I'm gunna stand here, gawping,' I say.

'Marvellous. Bloody marvellous,' sarcastic, but not necessarily annoyed.

'You haven't matched it right – over there.'

'Nobody's gunna get off a galloping horse to look at *that*, are they? Miss Perfect... Anyway, I haven't finished yet; hardly started. It won't notice.'

'I noticed.'

'You would,' she says, flat and crabby.

'Where's Dan?'

'In the shed.'

'In the shed?'

'That's what I said...'

'What doing?'

'How should *I* know. Doin' whatever it is that men do in sheds, I s'pose. Loves it in there, or seems to.'

'P'raps he's reading a mucky book...'

'P'raps he is.'

'P'raps he can't stand the sight of you any more...'

'P'raps he can't.'

'What's he gunna *say* when he comes in?'

She shrugs. 'Hang around and you'll find out. Mind you – he's been missing an hour and a half.

28

Could be in there all night.'

'Could be dead.'

'Could be. Wouldn't worry *you*, would it?'

'No, not much.'

'No love lost there . . .'

'You still gunna marry 'im, then, or what?'

'Never said I was, did I?'

'You did – once.'

'Can't remember saying that. Anyway, what for?' she says.

'You're engaged.'

'So?'

'Just asking . . .'

'*Shit*,' she says, screwing up the soggy mess in front of her. 'Shit, bugger, damn.'

'*Language*,' I say. 'You'll never go t' Heaven if you swear, y'know. They told us that at Primary.'

'Don't want t' go t' Heaven,' she says, ' – not with all them do-gooders. I want t' go to . . . Tenerife, or some-where.' Stands there, staring. Sighs. 'I hate *papering*. Never goes right. Never as easy as you thought.' Then, 'Want a drink?'

'What sort of drink?'

'A wet one, course.'

'Okay.'

She rinses her hands, managing to find the sink under the debris.

One of the earliest memories I've got is of me and Mum at the sink. Her flannelling me down on the cold metal draining board. Standing me up, bare bum pressing against the window pane. Then sitting me back down again, rubbing at me neck, trying to get the 'tide mark' off. And then getting the cloth between each toe,

29

really rough. Me hollering...

She makes coffee. Half filling two shiny purple mugs. Only ever get half a cup with Mum.

'Careful the wind don't change,' she says, ' – or your face'll stay like that.'

'Like what?'

'Like *that*. Miserable as sin.'

'I'm all right.'

'*I'm all right*,' she mocks. 'You don't look it. Look really peaky. Why's that?'

'I dunno.'

'*I dunno*,' she mocks again. 'Man trouble, is it?'

'No.'

'You haven't said much about 'im lately.'

'Nothin' t' say.'

'Used t' be all I ever heard – Liam this, Liam that.'

I give her a look.

'So? Just 'cause you don't like 'im.'

'I never said no such thing. What I said was – he's a bit of a *mystery*. Can't seem to get more than two words out of 'im.'

'Immature, you said.'

'Yeh...'

'And can't string a sentence together.'

'Well, he can't, can he? Not that I've heard. Just grunts at me.'

'He doesn't *grunt*.'

'Does.'

'*Doesn't*. You don't even *know* him.'

'Don't get the chance to...'

She casts her eyes down the garden for any sign of Dan. Nothing.

'You can tell me, y'know. I am your mother.'

'Tell you what?'

She hesitates.

'Whatever you want. There's something...something that's bothering you. I've noticed, just lately.'

I feel sick. What've I got – a neon advert on me forehead, or somethin'? Flashing lights announcing impending gloom and desperation?

'I'm all right.'

But me eyes start to swim, go all blinky and won't stop.

'Another girl, is it?' she says. ''Cause if it is...' She moves towards me but we don't touch. We never touch. 'Come on,' she says, uncomfortable. 'Can't be that bad.' I search for a hanky in me pocket. 'If he's messing around with somebody else... dump him, sharpish. Because they never change, y'know. And I speak from bitter experience.'

'It's not another girl,' I say. Dab me eyes. Wipe me nose.

'What is it, then?'

'Nothing.'

'*Rubbish.*'

'*There's nothing.*'

'Come on,' she says, acting all pally and upbeat. 'Now, let's see – if it's not man trouble...You're not ill, as such ...It can't be drugs 'cause you're not that stupid...' Then, 'You're *not*...?' She goes to joke, half laughing. 'You're *not*?' Like she doesn't dare say the word, but is still not serious. Looks at me. I turn away. 'Are you?' she says. Stops again. Then, 'Well, *are* you?' I don't answer. 'Well, say no, or say *something.*'

We stand there – her looking at me, me looking at the ceiling, at the walls, at the floor.

'Oh, for God's sake,' she says. 'I can't believe this. Are you telling me...' She doesn't finish the sentence. 'I mean ...'

She squashes the milk carton closed. Throws the teaspoon into the bowl. In a bit of a state, cardboardy and animated.

'*Say something*,' she says. '*Please*.'

I don't say anything for a bit. Still standing there. Then, 'What am I gunna do, Mum?' It comes out dead quiet and squeaky, not my voice at all.

She lights a cigarette.

'Oh, hell,' she says. 'Hell's bloody bells.' It's quiet and unreal.

Then, 'Let's go and sit down,' she says. 'In the other room.'

I can't believe she's not going mad. Not banging her fist on the table or strutting around, throwing her hands in the air.

She's just sat there. Staring at the carpet and chewing her lips. Her expression held firm.

And I'm sat there, picking at me nails, pulling at the skin that doesn't want to come away. And slowly, choking. Trying to swallow me feelings.

Then she starts crying, softly, just a bit.

I wish she'd stop. I'd rather somebody be angry than be upset. I'd rather she slapped me; it'd hurt less.

'Well,' she says, getting herself together. 'We'll sort something out...'

I say nothing. She starts to speak, but changes her mind, stops.

'I don't know what t' do,' I say.

'We'll sort it out,' she almost butts in, firmly this time. 'You're not the first and you won't be the last.'

32

Silence again.

I can't believe it. *Her.* I can't believe she's being . . . like I never would have thought . . .

'What's the man himself got t' say about it?'

'Doesn't know yet. Haven't told him. Haven't told anyone.'

She sighs.

'What d'you *think* he'll say?'

I shrug.

'Dunno.'

'Well, you never know,' she says. 'I mean, they're not all like your father. Presumably.' Then, all in a hurry, 'If I was you,' she says, 'I wouldn't let on to anybody else, not just yet. Not till you've made your mind up what t' do. There's no point giving people somethin' to gas about . . .' Looks awkward. 'It's nothin' much, not in the early stages – if you decide you don't want t' go through with it. I mean, you're not far gone, are you?'

But I've already decided.

'I'm keeping it.'

And she doesn't question my decision. Though the decision made itself; it's just the way I feel.

She nods, slowly.

'So long as you're sure,' she says.

'I'm sure,' I say.

I've surprised meself by telling her, first.

It's not like me and Mum have been close, not since Dan came on the scene.

I can't stand Dan; for the way he messed things up between us. I couldn't take to him, from the start. Though he'd say *wouldn't.* He didn't like me, either. That was obvious.

And Mum chose Dan over me – 'cause he could give her what she wanted; a better life. But lately, it doesn't look so good for her, not from where I'm standing.

Thinking over what she said, I can't help but wonder – if she ever regretted having me. Wished she hadn't . . .

I can hear Dan, outside, now.

Tell her I've got to get going.

'Don't go yet,' she says. 'There's no need.'

'What, with Dan coming in? You're optimistic . . .' I say.

'Don't worry about him,' she says. 'We've got things to . . . talk about. I mean, how you gunna . . . cope? What's gunna happen?'

I pull me coat round and stand up. 'You can't go – not yet,' she says.

'I'll see you again soon,' I say.

'When . . . ?'

I shrug.

'I've got t' get things straight, in me head.'

'Well listen, phone me, okay? And come round – in the week. Promise . . .' I sort of nod. Then, 'When you gunna tell him?' she says.

'Soon,' I say.

Then she nearly ruins everything.

'Well – let me know how the little snot takes it,' nasty like, '. . . and what part he intends to play in all of this.'

But I know her; I'm used to her and I let it go.

Then Dan comes in through the back door, steps straight into the bowl of paste.

'What the bloody hell's happening in 'ere?'

We both manage to grin; she crosses her fingers behind her back. Time for exit.

★

34

I walk home – the whole three miles trying to convince meself, believe that Liam'll stand by me. We'll be together. He's not me dad, after all. He's someone different; better.

When I get back to Evelyn's I'm glad to find an empty house; both of them out.

I look at the book again.

Try and work out how big the baby is. How much of a person it is already.

Then, in the morning – early – I make an excuse to go out; say I want somethin' from down the Spar shop; a packet of Polos and some crisps. Go over to the phone box and ring the doctor's.

I think about buying one of them home tests, but there's no point really – I already know what it'll say. And I can't afford to, anyway; they're about ten quid or something – I looked at them in Boots.

So, when I go to the appointment, they say they'll do their own test and I have to wee in this container – so they can send it off to be checked out.

He makes me feel too young and too clumsy, the doctor. Embarrassed and thick.

Asks, matter of fact, if I want the baby.

I tell him – I definitely want the baby.

Four

The whole thing just about blows Sarah's brains out.

Doesn't know what to say to start with. Can't get her head around it.

'Up the duff?! What – you're *sure*?'

'Yeh, course I'm sure.'

'For *certain*?'

'Certain.'

'*Bloody hell* . . . !' Then, 'And you're definitely having it?'

'Yeh.'

'What – *definitely*? You're . . .' She doesn't finish.

Silence.

Then she fires a zillion and one questions at me, one after another, till me head aches: What will you do? Where will you live? How will you manage? When is it due? What about Liam?

And I answer as best I can, not sure about most things

– but convinced I am doing right.

'I think you're...mad,' she says. Though doesn't try and change me mind.

Seems like a bit of an unfunny joke, to her.

But I know what Gran'd say; what she's said to me a hundred times before: just be true to yourself. No need to explain, no need to justify.

'I mean...I don't mean...What I mean is...'she's going.

'Sarah...' I say.

'Yeh...?'

'Shut up – before I kill you.'

'Sorry,' she says, and we laugh.

Her shock slipping away – she goes daft and normal.

'I can't imagine you, fat,' she says, as if that's the hardest part by far. *The* major concern.

'You'll be telling me I'll get big blue veins in me legs next,' I say.

'No, you won't,' she says. 'More *purple*. All knotty and throbbing!'

'Corned beef legs?!'

'Ugh...do you have to?!' she says. 'I'll probably get corned beef for me tea tonight...'

'Think of me while you're chewing on the gristle...' I say.

'*Ugh*...!' she squeals.

And I'm glad to be daft and normal, having a laugh. Gives me a break. Lets me breathe again for a while. Lets me feel – almost – excited. Then guilty, like I'm not allowed to be.

'I wonder what it is,' she says.

'A boy or a girl, I hope.'

'What you gunna call it?'

37

I shrug.

'Chloe, Zoe...'

'Ricky, Micky... Mabel.'

'Ken, Len, Den...'

'Doris, Maurice, Boris...'

'Bert the squirt.'

'Erik the Viking.'

'Alfred the Great.'

'You've got t' tell him,' she says.

'I will. Soon.'

'How soon?'

'Soon, soon.'

'Tonight, soon?'

'Maybe.'

'Definitely?'

'Definitely, maybe.'

'Promise? Before Evelyn susses you out?'

'We'll see.'

'You've got to tell him,' she says.

I don't go the long route home from Sarah's mum's; more like the completely-opposite-direction route. Via anywhere you care to mention.

Eventually, when I get there, Liam's in a good mood.

Upstairs, changing. Damping his hair down, brushing his teeth.

'Fancy a curry tonight?' he gurgles through a gobful of Macleans. Me mouth waters, in pre-vomit anticipation.

'*Curry?*'

'Don't say it like that. *It's pay day!*' Spitting the paste into the grubby basin and taking a gulp from the plastic beaker on the side. Wiping his mouth with the towel and leaving a minty-white stain, as usual.

'How much did you get this week?'

'Mind your own...' tapping the side of his nose with his finger.

I try and concentrate on anything bar a meat vindaloo and bhindi bhajee.

'Bit of a waste of money.'

'Who says? It's not. Let's go out – have a good time, for a change.'

'I thought we were saving. We need loads just for a deposit.'

He looks put out. Looks at me the way you look at your mother or something, when she's giving you grief about sod all.

'I'm not putting it *all* back, *every* week. I'll see what I've got left over, come next Thursday. I want t' *enjoy meself*.'

'You won't have *any* left by next Thursday, though, will you?'

He just shrugs.

'Have to see, won't we?'

'You can go...' I say, 'if you want to. I'm not fussed.'

'I don't want t' go *on me own*, do I?'

'See if Paul's about then.'

'He'll be skint, always is. *What's up with you, anyway?*'

'I just don't feel like it, that's all.'

'You're no fun, you mean. You're *boring*.' But he's not riled or anything.

He turns the tap on, full blast. Splashes his face.

Still wet, starts larking around – flicking water at me. Then comes over, tries to hold me down on the bed t' tickle me; blow a raspberry on me bare stomach.

'Get off!'

'Make me…' Wrestling some more.

'Get off me! I *mean* it…!'

'No…!'

'You're *soaking*…'

'So?'

'It's… horrible. Stop it! *Liam!*'

'What?'

'*Listen*…'

'Yeh…?'

'*Listen*…' I gasp and he stops; sits up, grinning.

'What…?'

I don't say anything.

'Well, I'm listening…' Swaying back and forth.

'I've got somethin' t' tell you.'

'Yeh,' he goes, still joky.

And I say it. Shaking. Almost a whisper.

'I'm pregnant.'

He stops dead.

'*What?*'

He's still as a statue; as if one of us has lost the plot.

Still quietly, I say it again.

'*I'm pregnant.*'

Silence.

'You can't be,' disbelieving.

'Why not?'

Another silence.

'You *can't be.*'

He gets up. Is staring into the sink now, leaning on either side.

And I'm waiting.

And he doesn't say – don't worry, it'll be all right. He

40

doesn't say – we'll be okay, come here. Doesn't say anything. Anything at all. Slowly puts the towel to his face to dry.

'Two and a half months,' I say.

'Shut up,' he cuts in. 'Just shut up a minute.'

I'm panicking.

He drops the towel, is hanging his head, clasping and twisting his hands. Looking around. Looking angry. And the knot inside of me is hurting.

He sits down on the bed again.

Both of us sitting there. Me, too scared to speak. Make a move. A movement.

'*For fuck's sake*,' he says. 'How did you manage *that*?'

'*Me?*' I say.

All of a sudden, there's the thud of feet on the stairs, a loud bang on the bedroom door.

'What y' up to in there? *Disgusting*...'

It's Rob, one of his cronies.

A couple of seconds pass.

'Come in, mate,' he calls back, his voice not quite right – maybe a bit strained – but more or less okay. Rob bursts in.

'What's goin' on then?'

'Nothin' much.'

'Not *interrupting* anything, am I?'

'I should be so lucky... Nah – you're sound...'

'You've either been shagging or rowing,' he says. 'I can tell.'

'Yeh, well. Something like that...'

'Coming out to play tonight, then?' Rob carries on. 'Or won't the missus let you?' They both laugh at the thought, but Liam has to force it out.

'Twist me arm...'

'A pint and a game of pool?'

'Only if you insist...'

'I insist. Best get dressed, son. Wasting good time.' He looks over. 'All right, female?'

I throw him a look. Prat.

'Quiet tonight?'

'Nothin' t' say,' I tell him.

'Unusual, for a woman,' he says. 'They've usually got plenty t' say.'

'But nothin' we want t' hear,' Liam says and I feel like smacking him one.

Rob grins. 'Like that, is it?'

'Get lost,' I mutter, to neither one in particular; the pair of them.

Liam pulls on a tee shirt and a clean pair of jeans. Combs his hair. Laces his trainers.

'Coming?' Rob asks me.

'No, she's stopping in,' Liam answers. 'We'll go by ourselves. Up for a curry, later?'

'Sounds good,' Rob says. 'Very good...'

As they leave, Liam glares at me; empty. Like he despises me.

'Don't wait up. We'll be late.' Slams the door.

I go to the window. Watch them, outside. Mucking around and laughing like kids. Strutting along the street as if they own every filthy inch of it. And I hurt. *It just wasn't meant to be like this.* But I don't know what t' do about it.

There're lots of little Liams and Robs playing outside. Football, mostly; with a bit of wrangling now and then – nippers turning nasty.

42

This is a so-called good road; meaning on the edge of the estate – not slap bang in the middle – not mentioned in the local rag quite as often as some. Just an ordinary hole. With so-called ordinary people doing so-called ordinary things. Existing, on the edge.

If we could get out of here, on our own . . . If we could get away from this place – his stupid pals and stupid mother, make the break . . .

I want Liam to meself. But can't seem to make it happen.

And I want me gran. But can't make that happen, either.

What would she say now – me gran? I mean, I know what Mum'd say – she'd get on her high horse, give him a gobful of abuse and a fistful of knuckles. But me gran?

She'd say – stop your crying, for a start. She'd say – I don't like t' see you cry.

And then she'd probably say, give him some time. To let it sink in. She'd say – it's not so simple, after all; a big thing to take on board. Give him the benefit of the doubt, for now. Give him a chance.

No, she wouldn't.

She'd *demolish* him. He wouldn't know what'd hit him – his head in January, his arse in September.

But I'm not like me gran. I've got t' cling on and give him that chance.

Liam's the only person that's ever made me feel good. Because of Liam, I belonged. And all I want is for him to love me back. I've got to *try*. Not just for me, but for our baby, too.

Evelyn calls out,

'Come and get your washing – me kitchen's like a damn laundry again.'

And I think, you ain't seen nothin' yet, love – 'cause if we don't find a place, soon...

I go down and get our clean things, stiff from the radiator.

'The heating doesn't work proper if you cover it with clothes,' she says. 'And it could start a fire.'

'There's only hot water inside...'

'There's a *risk* – somebody said.'

And I feel like saying – who? Who said? Liar.

I ask if it's okay to have a bath.

'So long as you don't use all the hot water; tidy up after yourself. And don't use my flannel...'

Oh, stuff off, Evelyn.

She goes out to bingo.

I have a long, deep soak in peace. 'Cept for the noise of the squabbling and squealing going on next door, but I'm used to that. Bubbles galore, in this vile turquoise and peach wonderland. Eyes closed, trying to let me mind wander. But it won't.

I slide me fingers and palm over me wet tum. Still flat. Flat as a pancake. Though not for much longer.

Go to bed, early.

I only know Liam is home when I hear him being sick.

He sleeps beside me like a dead man.

In the morning, we ignore each other, bar the odd word and gesture. He's propped in front of the portable like a sack of spuds, watching cartoons, bleary eyed.

I want to leave him to stew, but at the same time, I don't. I want him to talk to me.

And he does open his mouth, eventually.

'What you gunna do?' he says.

'God, it's still got a pulse, then...' I say.

Then, I tell him. I'm going to have the baby.

'And anyway,' I say. 'Don't you mean – what're *we* gunna do? It's *your* baby, too.'

He's slumped there, motionless, except for when he swigs from his can of fizzy orange. Doesn't answer for a minute. Then, 'How do I know it's mine?' he says.

Y'see, Liam can make me feel good, like no one else can. Or Liam can make me feel like dirt.

Five

'Get rid of it,' Evelyn says, from her soap box on the ceiling. Then, 'I can understand anyone making a mistake, but what I can't understand is – what you think you have to offer a child.'

And Liam says, 'I can't handle all this. It's doin' my head in.' Which is very damn helpful, very damn typical.

I walk out.

Mel reckons everyone'll 'get used' to the idea. Including Liam. But I don't want him to just 'get used' to it; that's not exactly what you'd call *commitment*, is it? I want him to *want* it.

She seems sure; says, 'Don't worry, he'll come round.'

'But what if he gives you an ultimatum?' Sarah pipes up, unconvinced. 'Him or the baby – what'll you do then?'

'She might *want* him,' Mel says, 'but it doesn't

necessarily mean she *needs* him.'

So many people trying to decide my life; all with their own version of what's right.

Sarah stays quiet as I go through it all again – what's been said – by Mum, Liam, Evelyn –what *I* think, what *I* want. But I'm so freaked out, inside, I'm getting so confused...

'You just have to get through it,' Mel says. 'It'll be okay.'

'But are you *really* sure, it's what you want?' Sarah chips in.

'Course she is,' Mel says.

Mel starts talking about Zac.

About his dad.

Mel and him don't live together but, 'I'm still seeing him,' she says. Sighs. 'You just have to get on with it. It's hard sometimes – but it's not all bad. I've got no regrets. Well, maybe a few.'

'Like what?' I ask. But she doesn't seem to know.

'Freedom...?' Sarah says.

'Not exactly,' Mel answers, thinking about it. '*Time*. I'd like more time for meself and more patience for Zac – I'd like to shout less and not get so stressed out.'

'I've never heard you shout,' I say.

'Just because you haven't heard me,' she says, 'doesn't mean it never happens. I get so... frustrated. Wish I could get away now and then. But unless you've got help – or can *afford* help, you're always needed.'

'That's what I said,' Sarah pipes up. '*Freedom*.'

'Maybe...' Mel says.

'Would you like a job?' I say. 'If you could get someone t' have him?'

'Being a mum *is* a job,' she says. Then, 'Yeh. Course I

would. But I try not to dream – that way, you don't get disappointed. I wouldn't earn enough to pay a babysitter…'

'When we were younger,' Sarah says, 'you always reckoned you were gunna be an *air hostess*,' putting on a posh accent.

'Oh, yeh – sure,' Mel winces, embarrassed. 'Some hopes. That was then, this is now.'

Mel's right about one thing though – Liam does seem to have 'come round'.

I mean, he's not exactly jumping for joy – he's still moody; his head seems to be somewhere else – but at least we're talking now; whereas we haven't been.

'Me mum took it well, didn't she?' he says, taking the rise. Almost – I think – apologising for her? Well, at least not defending her.

'Crabby cow,' I say, and he smiles.

The atmosphere is weird. We're awkward together. Feelings putting a distance between us. But at least he's making an effort.

'Me old man'd be happy,' he says. 'But then, he'd be happy whatever was goin' on – 'cause being alive's generally better than being dead. He always said he wanted a grandson, though.'

'Might be a girl,' I say.

'Nah – it's a boy.'

'How d'you know?'

'I just do. I'm tellin' you – it's a lad.'

He sounds almost pleased, I think.

'*You* don't think I should get rid of it then…?'

'I don't know what I think. I think it's up to you. If you want it…'

'But what do *you* want?'

'Does it matter,' he says, 'what *I* want?'

'Yes … And no.'

'There you go, then; there's your answer. You've already made up your mind.'

He puts his arm round my shoulder, and it feels heavy and welcome. Takes a cigarette from the pack of ten in his top pocket. Lights up. Doesn't offer me one; not out of concern – he never offers.

'I know what me gran'd say,' I tell him.

'What's that?'

'*Worse things 'appen at sea.*' One of her gems. He half smiles.

'Do they? Like what, I wonder?' Takes a deep drag.

It's funny, how quickly things can change. Not long ago, I was living with Gran; had never even heard of Liam. Didn't know he existed.

When I took him home to meet her – a while before she got taken poorly – her only comment was, '… and I don't trust that good-looking bugger, either…' That's about the best I could have expected from Gran. She sort of meant it, but didn't really. I think she liked him well enough. More than Mum did, anyhow. *She* made herself more than clear – left him in no doubt.

'S'pose *your* mother blames me?' he says.

'Dunno, really…'

'Huh…' he goes, like it's inevitable.

Mum was so chuffed, last year, when she found *she* was expecting. Singing in the street, practically. I was jealous. Dead jealous. Thought she wouldn't want to know me at all when she had her baby. *Dan's* baby. Then she lost it, miscarried. No reason, it just happened. She was dead upset for ages. I didn't know whether to mention it, or not. If she wanted me to, or not. I don't know how I'd feel, if anything went wrong with my baby, now. Like, no one thinks I've got the right to be happy about having it. But I do love it, already. And if I lost it, it'd be awful. Though still, somehow, probably, a relief. I'm no less scared now than I ever have been.

'We'll have t' get some money together,' I say. 'And I thought *I* might be able to get *something* – part time. Down the shops, stacking shelves, maybe…Evenings. I've seen them advertise before now.'

'No one'll take you on now,' he says. 'That's a dead end.'

'They might…'

Then, 'I might be able to pick something else up,' he says. 'Something better, more pay…'

'D'you think so? D'you think you could?'

He shrugs.

'Dunno. We can't live here,' he says. 'I couldn't stand it. There's no room as it is.'

'And Evelyn'd stick her oar in…'

'She won't want us here, that's a cert.'

'Did she say?'

'Didn't have to.'

'Can you imagine – the baby dribbling and whatnot over her stuff. She'd rather die.'

'It's all she's got, this place,' he says, a bit irritated, defending her again. 'And she worked hard for it.'

'I heard, she got most of it from the catalogue and never even paid for it…'

'You don't know that,' he says. 'Stop bitching.'

I drop it, mustn't start anything, even if I'm right.

'Did you tell the gang?' I ask. 'Your mates?'

'Told a couple – so they all know by now.'

'What did they say?'

'Laughed, mostly,' he says. 'Peed themselves, in fact. Wouldn't believe me to start.'

I pull a face; who cares what they think?

'We'd best buy the paper this Friday,' I say. 'See what flats are going.'

'Not much point – we can't afford it yet.'

'You never know…'

'I *know*. And we can't afford it.'

'But there's nothing t' stop us *looking*.'

'What's the *point*?' he says, getting uptight. 'Don't start going on about it, 'cause that's what really gets to me – when you go on and on and on about things.'

Part Two

Part Two

Six

I've tried not to 'go on about things'. All the way through, and it's been all right most of the time. Though I wish I could speak me mind – say what *I* think – without it causing a ruck.

But six months down the line we're still together, at least. Nothing much has changed – not for Liam anyway – he still goes out with his mates and all that. I stay in; get tired. He doesn't understand that.

'You've been sat on your backside doing nothin' all day...' Which isn't true – I do me bit, around the house and that. But according to Liam, work with no money attached isn't proper work.

It's not like I haven't tried to find a job. But I can't do anything now, not till the baby's born. I'd like to get something. And I know I *will*, eventually. Though I wish I had...more bottle...It's just, I can't seem to face it, push meself forward any more. I feel nervous and hopeless and a fool up against other people. Up against Liam sometimes, too.

I pretend to be asleep when he comes home. It's easier that way.

Though he's been really wary of me – ever since the bump started to show. And now –

'Looks like an alien – trying to fight its way out,' he says, as I'm stretched out on the bed in all me glory. 'It's…ugh…'

'Thank you very much,' I say, sharp.

'Only joking…' he says. Says I take too much to heart.

It's all right for him. Fact is, *I'm* the size of a small hot-air balloon.

Nearly there, now.

He doesn't like to see the baby move inside of me. Says the first time it happened, it made him want to heave.

'It's freaky. Not normal.' Turns his face away. 'Cover it up.'

Mind you, it made *me* feel funny, queasy to start with – when it moved – but now I don't mind being prodded and kicked in the ribs. Means that everything's all right. I tell him so.

'All right?' he says. 'Sure. We're the luckiest people alive,' dead sarky.

Though there have been times when he's seemed excited, proud even. A new life and all that. His own child…a little Liam…But then there's times when he's been really down – feeling the weight of it all. Mostly, he's tried to ignore it, forget it, I know.

We're still at Evelyn's, see. It's not going so well and he acts like it's my fault. Says it's harder to get a place when you've got a kid on the way; nobody's interested – in case they can't get you out if you don't pay up. He says he's doing his best, trying to find somewhere. I say, sometimes his best isn't good enough. I say, let's rely on winning the Lottery, it'll come quicker. Then there's a barney. So we've stopped talking about it, lately. Only makes for a scene.

We're just drifting on – just letting things happen – as if one day, someone's gunna tap on the door – say, here, have this super-duper luxury apartment – take it, it's yours. As if.

It's not that I want anything fancy. Just *something*. *Somewhere*.

Sometimes I wonder, what's really going on, inside his head.

When I think back, to when we first met – it seems like a thousand years ago; even though it's little more than a year.

When we used to be out and about, messing around, having the laugh of all laughs. Night after night.

But it's just not like that any more.

'Baby, baby, baby,' he says. 'That's all you think about. You haven't got a life any more. You're not *you* any more.'

I try to explain – the responsibility I feel. Try to tell him, 'Once I've had it, we'll…'

But he cuts me short.

'Yeh,' he says. 'I know…' Not giving me a chance. Not believing anything will ever be different. Better.

I didn't know how much things would change, either. They have – and I can't help it. They're going to – and I can't help it. But it doesn't mean we won't ever have good times again, does it?

All I know is – I really want this baby.

I look at the scan picture – pinned on our wall. And I can't believe it. I must have looked at it a million times. Liam says it looks like a long-range weather forecast to him; can't make head nor tail of it. He says he can't imagine –

'…what he'll be like.' Still insisting it's a boy.

'Or what *she'll* be like,' I say, for the hundredth time.

You can't tell if it's a boy or a girl from the scan photo – like, it's not obvious or anything. I could've asked, but I didn't. I want to wait. And once it's born, he'd better love it whatever it is.

'It's a *boy*,' he says. 'And it's about time you bought him his first Tottenham shirt.'

Mum says it's about time Liam pulled his finger out and did something useful.

'…about time he grew up.'

I try not to get into it with her – like, no way will I take her side, against Liam. She shouldn't expect me to, either – I mean, look at her and Dan – didn't want to know what I thought of him, did she? Shouldn't put me on the spot, but she does. Forever pointing out – 'what his trouble is…', and predicting what he'll do next, like she's some psychic or other: 'Course – you know what'll happen…' she starts, 'I'm telling you now…' Makes me more determined to make it work – prove her wrong. Like, I *know* what I've gotten meself into, I don't need telling. But I've not got much in the way of options right now. I'm not an idiot – *I've just got to try and make it work*.

Still. I don't gloat when she announces in some stressed–out manic babble that Dan's 'an ignorant pig who can't even flush the loo or change his pants' without her help. Or say anything – much – when she says, '…and I *know* he's not been working late.' I merely *suggest*:

'Kick him out.'

She looks shocked.

'Don't be ridiculous,' she says. 'It's not *that* bad. I didn't mean…' Then, 'I can't, can I?' she says. 'Everything's in his name. Some things, you just have to learn to live with. You'll soon find that out.'

Says if *they'd* had a baby, everything might've settled. Might've made them closer. But instead – he's only got his son 'from *her*' – his last girlfriend.

'But you don't think it'll make me and Liam closer…?'

'I don't know,' she says. 'You're young. It's different.'

Mum hates having Dan's kid there, every weekend. Says it's like having her nose rubbed in it.

I build up the courage to ask her about losing her baby. It upsets her. Says she wanted that baby, desperately.

And that Dan couldn't handle it – didn't know how. But wasn't so much grieved as embarrassed. Because they'd told everyone and then had to go round un-telling everyone. He felt a fool.

I embarrass Liam. If we're out, he walks on, in front of me. Makes out he's on his own. Says he doesn't, but he does.

In a minute, she starts back-pedalling – saying it's just a bad patch they're going through right now, a phase. That she knows he wants it to work as much as she does.

'Can't be lovey-dovey all the time,' she says. So there. Suddenly – Dan the Man works hard, deserves a break, is second only to Mr Jesus Christ and eveything's her fault.

'It's just that…' She shrugs. 'I'm used to being let down. Expect it.'

She gives me a bag of stuff she'd bought for their baby. Vests, a little jacket, a minuscule pair of jeans. The ones she brought to show me, in the café, when she told me she was pregnant. It brings it back to me – how cut up I felt. How screwed up – at the thought of her having another kid – one she might want, more than she wanted me.

'I hung on to them,' she says. 'Don't know why. Just couldn't bring meself to get rid of them at the time.'

They're cute and real and scary.

'You might need them,' I say.

'No,' she says. 'I won't need them,' and I wish I hadn't said it.

Mum's got this way of making me feel sorry for her. Like, no matter how much we bicker or fall out – I still want to make it better for her, protect her. And I still want her approval.

Gran used to say, 'She can turn it on and off like a light switch. Don't be taken in.'

But I just worry. That she's getting to be this sad, used, chewed up woman, and not the one she could be, if things were different.

'Don't worry about *her*,' Liam says. 'Shit happens – to everyone.'

He comes in, casually, with the news –

'Got another job.'

'Another job?'

'That's what I said.'

'What – a better job?'

'A different job.'

'What's that meant to mean?'

60

'Do I have to spell everything out for you? It means — a different job,' he says. Then, under his breath, 'Think yourself lucky I've got a job at all.'

Apparently, he's going to be 'all over the place', 'helping this bloke', as a driver's mate — delivering, collecting, bit of this, bit of that. Says, eventually, he might even get to drive, '…and there's big money in that; loads of fiddles, too.' Says he told them to stick the poxy labouring job where the sun don't shine — find some other clown to do it.

He looks at me.

'Don't worry,' he says. I put me hand out and we link fingers for a second. 'It's gunna be all right,' he says. Then pulls back.

It turns out that he does get a bit more money. But not much; a few quid. And it's longer hours, so I see even less of him; more of Evelyn. Who, when the mood takes her, seems to forget I've been up and down doing all sorts, and all but accuses me of being the laziest human being alive. Snorting things like, 'Pregnancy isn't an *illness*, y'know.' I could *deck her*, sometimes.

Liam's vague — about times, about where he's going to be working; says he doesn't know *every detail*. And vague about where he's been. Says he shouldn't have to report back *every detail*.

It's like I'm asking him to disclose some high-risk republican plot to assassinate the monarchy or something. But I'm just *interested*, that's all. I just like to know — it's *conversation*, something to talk about. *I* haven't got much to talk about — he doesn't want to hear about the baby all the time, and whatever else I say always seems to be wrong. Or boring.

61

He says I want to 'know it all' because I don't trust him – and that I ought to learn, before he gets so hacked off he can't stand it any more.

'And, no – ' he says, 'before you ask again – you *can't* have any more money *for the baby*. The sooner you come back down to earth the better.'

Evelyn offers me a pair of old blue sheets – says I can cut them up, hem them, for the cot.

'Put 'em through the boil wash – they'll be perfectly all right. Perfectly adequate. And beggars can't be choosers.' Never mind I haven't *got* a cot, yet.

I need *things*. There's so much stuff – bottles, steriliser…loads of things.

I'm borrowing a lot from Liam's cousin, Tracey. It's *all right*, some of it. I try not to compare it to the crisp, new, boxed things I see in the shops. I want better for my baby, but I know I can't have it.

The trouble is, that when you *can't have it* – people look down on you.

And I'm fed up with everyone looking down on me. Specially the older, sorted Mums, like some of the ones at the clinic. I couldn't go to any more of the classes because of *them*. Could see it on their pearly lips – she's *young*, she's this, it's that. They make me feel so small. Like I can't possibly be as good a mother as they can.

But at the same time, deep down, I want to *be* those other women I see. I want their life, their home, their everything. For my baby. I want not to be stuck here.

I want to look like they look. Together and in control. Not be a fat, ugly blob with nothing to say. Maybe it's no wonder Liam's never at home.

Even Sarah's made comments. Remarks about how I

look, how I am. As if she's *stunning*; a vision of loveliness.

I think sometimes that she's jealous, in a way. Is bitching, because when the baby comes, I'll have something special, that she hasn't got. And wonder, too, if she doesn't fancy Liam herself, or somethin'.

And I will be a good mum – as good as the rest of them. Better even. Like Mel.

'You'll be fine,' she keeps telling me. 'Just you wait and see.'

I tell her – how I can hardly even turn over in bed any more.

'Normal…' she says. 'Along with a weak bladder and scrambled brains. Just normal…'

Then, 'Can I have a feel?' she says.

'D'you want to?'

I pull me shirt up. She rests her hand on the bare bump.

'Wow!' as the baby kicks. 'Look at him go!'

I wriggle about a bit. 'Feels like he's wedged sideways…' Then, 'Did your belly get itchy?' I ask her.

'Pl-eeease,' Sarah groans.

'Itchy? Are you kidding? It was like I had fleas, burrowing away,' Mel says.

'P'raps you did,' Sarah grunts.

'P'raps…'

She gives me a bin liner full of Zac's old things – different outfits; mostly snagged and faded, but trendy, the sort of stuff I'd like to buy. And bright-coloured plastic toys that sing and ring and rattle; drive you nuts.

'Everything's clean,' she says. 'But you'll need to press the clothes.'

We wade through it all. Pulling things out and holding them up.

'Aahhh, look…'

'Look at this… It's so cute.'

'So tiny…'

'Babies are,' Mel says.

'But big enough,' Sarah says. 'When you think where they have to come from.'

'Shut up,' Mel says.

'It's true…'

'You'll be all right,' she says to me.

'It's not *that* bad, is it?' I say.

'If it was *that bad*, nobody'd ever have more than one, would they?'

'You haven't…' Sarah says.

'You know what I mean,' she says.

'You've changed your tune, Mel,' she says. 'What did you say? Think of the worst pain you can possibly imagine – then double it?'

'Shut up,' she says. 'You just get through it. Everyone does.'

'Mel was a day and a half in labour – forceps, stitches, the lot. They have to put your legs up in these…'

'Sarah! Shut it, okay?'

Seven

The pains start in the morning, just after I get up. Not bad, but more than just twinges. Like, I know something's going on, something's moving.

I time how far apart they are; all over the place – ten minutes, fifteen, four…two, twenty. I feel scared, but on top of it.

Liam's at work. Evelyn tells me to sit with me feet up; generous, I think. She seems to believe I've got a nasty case of wind or something. Offers me a mint.

'That'll clear it. It won't be the baby – you're not due yet, and I doubt you'll be early. It's just your body, getting ready. Or anxiety – that's probably what it is.' She's all experienced and dismissive. No, she doesn't think I should 'bother' Mum. No, she certainly doesn't think I should 'bother' the hospital. 'Contact Liam at work? What for?' she says. 'Even if it *was* something – you'd have hours and hours to go yet,' dead smug, like. 'Put the telly on, take your mind off it.'

I sit and watch a programme about paint effects – sponging, ragging and bagging. And how to make swags and tails – 'transform your living space' – for a pound a metre.

She's hovering well enough, though. I wish she'd get lost if it's *nothing*.

'I wonder if they'll show *stencilling*?' she says. 'I'll hang about, just in case; wouldn't mind having a go at that.'

More like, she's worried me waters'll break on her sofa or some such tragedy, and she wants to be ready to mop up the stain, pronto.

And in a bit, I do try and phone Mum, from the call box across the road. Can't get hold of her. Don't know where she is.

And try to track Liam down. But nobody knows where he is, either. Not that he'd come until it's all over – he's already said as much.

I have something to eat, though I don't really want it. A KitKat and an egg sandwich. Evelyn complains that it stinks 'like elephant dung' – though how she knows, I'm not entirely sure.

I wander around, can't settle.

Check me bag, wanting to be ready, just in case. Feel meself working up into a state, now. Not knowing if I've got everything I need: babygrows, biscuits, bum cream. Nappies, nighties, knickers. Soft towels the size of a small child. Sanitary towels the size of a small town. Spot cream and an extra packet of coconut crunchies. I can't think straight...

The morning goes on and nothing happens. Evelyn loses interest.

'False alarm. Told you,' before disappearing upstairs to

fiddle with a pair of curtains.

'I wonder what it'd look like if I draped a length of net across the top – scooped it up at the ends?'

But by mid afternoon – no matter what she says – I'm in *no* doubt.

I'm forcing meself to concentrate on something – *anything* – the wastepaper bin, the standard lamp, a framed picture of the Pope...crossing me legs, pretending it's not happening – not yet, not today, maybe tomorrow...I'll be ready then, psyched up...But the pains are getting sharper-quicker-sharper-quicker and I'm getting just about frightened to death and here I am talking to him now, talking to the picture of the Pope, saying – pleeeease, *do* something, under me breath – and he's smiling back and waving and doing sod all.

I draw me legs up.

'*Evelyn...*'

And does she hammer down those stairs – go into overdrive, or what?

I want me mum, but she says we'd best get to the hospital first. I want Liam, but she says there's no point just yet. She wants to change her skirt. I want to change me mind.

'Keep yer chin up,' she says.

'It's not me *chin* I'm worried about...'

'You don't know anythin' yet, love...'

Someone said that an ambulance costs the best part of thirty quid, so she bangs up Wilf, next door. Says it's an emergency and all.

'Jesus...' he says. Funny – 'cause I'm talking to Him, too.

Somehow, I get bundled out the door and into his purple Escort van. He makes the sign of the cross on his chest; very reassuring, like.

'Don't bother with seat belts,' she's saying. 'I'll do the talking, if we get stopped.'

'Bugger the seat belts,' Wilf says, and drives like lightning, dead erratic; accelerating and braking hard; dodging in and out.

'Is this thing taxed, Wilf?' Evelyn asks.

'No,' he says, 'but *I* am. How about you love?' he says to me.

'Piss off,' I say, doubled up.

'*Charming.*'

He gets us there, somehow, with me still in one piece, though folded in two at times. I don't think I say 'thanks' or anything, though I notice the look of relief on his face.

Once inside, I burst into tears. People are looking. Staring. It smells – a disinfected hospitally smell, straight up your nose – though clean and fresh and airy. We take the lift to the top floor, Evelyn faffing, me whingeing and wincing.

'Can you let us in, please,' she says over the entry phone. Then, '*Bloody let us in!*' when nothing happens immediately.

The doors open. Everyone is smiley and in control. Kindly and calm. They ask who I am and take me notes. Show me to the ward and tell me to get undressed. Give me a starchy, cardboardy nightgown with Health Authority stamped all over it, blue and green and red.

The bed is hard.

'No panic,' Evelyn's saying, panicking. 'No need to panic.'

But I don't want her to talk. Don't want to listen. I only want to hit her.

The midwife comes and swishes the bright, tacky curtains round.

'Right. Let's have a little look then . . .'

Starts to examine me, dead gentle. But I hate it and I want to hit her, too.

'*Leave me alone!*'

'It's all right,' she says. 'Come on, it's all right.'

In a minute and probably to Evelyn's delight, she tells me there's 'some way to go, yet.' Then, 'Have you got a birth plan, love?' she asks.

Plan! As if.

I tell her, no. I tell her I'm scared. I tell her it's hurting.

She wheels over a canister on a trolley, puts a mask to me face.

'Gas and air . . .' she says. 'When you feel a contraction coming – breathe. It'll take the edge off the discomfort.'

Discomfort?! Hah, is that all it is?

I snatch the mask and breathe. Me head goes floaty. I breathe harder. And harder and harder.

'Greedy!' she says, smiling again. Is talking about 'other forms of pain relief.'

'I want it all,' I say. 'And I want it now,' scared half to death.

Then, 'Let's have a look at the monitor,' she says, almost to herself. Straps a widish piece of elastic round me middle. Fiddles and farts around, looking, listening.

'Is everything all right?' Evelyn's going. 'Is everything okay?'

'Yes,' she says. 'Everything's fine. No problems.' Then, at last, 'I'll nip and get you something.'

Comes back with a syringe that can't possibly be big enough. Gives me an injection.

'It's not working,' I say. 'It's no better.'

'Give it a chance!' she says.

And in a while, the pain starts to dull.

I feel ill. Dopey. Sleepy like a space man. Dreamy. Alone.

I want me gran. I want me mum. I want Liam. I feel sick. Drifting off. Still awake, but not *really* awake. Kind of aware of things happening around me for a while, then…nothingness.

When I come to again, it's to the sound – the noise – of clattering and clashing voices. I don't know how long I've been here. What time it is…or what day it is. But I'm still here and I don't much like it. It's hurting again. And the voices…

Evelyn. Mum.

'What d'you mean – you couldn't get in touch with me? Did you *try*?' Not giving Evelyn the opportunity to answer. 'And another thing,' she says, 'where's that lousy son of yours?'

'If it wasn't for *me*…' she starts to defend herself…

'*Excuse me*,' a voice butts in, 'please calm down, or we'll have to ask you to go outside – we can't have you upsetting the patients.'

Mum snorts. Evelyn protests her innocence.

'I fully agree…'

The curtain is scraped back.

'Love…' Mum says. 'How are you?'

I start to cry.

'I can't do this. Help me, Mum…'

'Yes, you can. Come on…' she says, putting her hand in mine as the next wave rolls over me. 'Blimey,' she says. 'Nearly squeezed the blood out of me fingers…Still, that's one less to go. One step closer,' she says.

'Does anyone want a hot drink?' Evelyn asks, spikily. 'Only I, for one, feel parched – and I think we're in for the night.'

They have a coffee. I have a catheter.

'They don't seem to do an enema these days,' Evelyn muses, disappointed. 'Personally, I think they ought to...'

'Not long now, love,' Mum is saying. 'Soon be over.'

'And we'll have a lovely bonny babe,' Evelyn adds, softening for the occasion.

It is long. Long, long, long – if you're *me*. Hours, hours, hours. And although Mum's with me, I'm still on me own. Completely on me own, inside. Reaching out, but nobody's there.

Eventually, when they've examined me again – decided that 'things are progressing nicely', they move me, wheel me away to somewhere else.

The delivery suite is a bit of a blur, even though the drugs have worn off and they won't let me have any more. There's a different nurse. Lots of scary equipment – big, bulky stuff like you see on the telly. There might be a sink in the corner, I'm not sure – but there's definitely a fan, whirring round, blowing cool air.

I'm tired. Dog tired. They put me on a drip. I don't know if it helps. I don't care what they do, by now. Can cut me head off with a chainsaw if they like. It's all unreal.

They have another poke around. I wish I was dead. They say everything's fine. I still wish I was dead.

'Let me die,' I say to them.

'Too much paperwork involved,' the nurse says.

Then the pace changes. Moves up a gear and they're telling me to breathe and push, and I'm breathing and pushing; telling me to pant and push, and I'm panting and pushing, panting and pushing.

'Come on,' they're saying. 'Good girl. Come on…'

Till I can feel it, I can really feel it coming…

Eventually, 'We can see the head…!' And with that, both Mum and Evelyn abandon me, rush to the bottom of the bed – neither wanting to be outdone.

'Nearly there…one big push…*come on*! That's it! That's lovely! Smashing – nearly there, now…'

And when the baby is born it's the most amazing, the most wonderful moment of my life.

The pain is gone; I don't care about anything – I am the happiest person alive.

I'm crying. Mum is crying. Evelyn is crying.

This little naked stranger plonked in me arms.

'A perfect little girl,' someone says. 'Isn't she just perfect?'

I've got a baby, a baby girl. And I'm so happy; I can't tell you how happy I am.

Studying her; the tiniest fingers and toes, her hair, her tiny nose, lips, eyes. The way she looks at me – I just can't explain.

'Whaaaa…!' she screams, and it's beautiful, just beautiful.

'I can't believe I'm a grannie,' Mum says, still weepy. 'Look at her – I can't believe it.'

And I'm a mum. I feel like a mum. I feel it stronger than I've ever felt anything before. My baby. *My baby*…I can't believe how lucky I am – just to have felt the moment.

She's so gorgeous; not crumpled or crinkled. Gorgeous – better than any baby I've ever seen.

They wrap her in a cotton shawl. She looks like a princess.

'Will somebody get Liam…?' I say.

Eight

I'm back on the ward, mid morning. They've given me a bath. Dressed the baby in a little white brushed gown, pink knitted cardi and bonnet. Given her back, gift wrapped and sound.

They've left me now, with a cup of weak tea, two paracetamols and a cottage cheese sandwich, which is gross, but it doesn't matter.

I keep the curtains pulled shut. Don't want to share my baby. I'm on me own with her and it's peaceful and special and I want to save this time forever.

'*Yee ha!*' Liam bursts in, throwing a bunch of crushed, raspberry red carnations on the bed, beaming, ear to ear, and smelling of beer.

'Look at her!' he says. '*Just-look-at-her!*' Loud and fake and full of it; showing off. 'She's really…nice,' he says.

'*Nice?* Is that all?'

'No – I mean…*really* nice.' Looks at her. '*Scary.*' Sits down, eyes fixed on the transparent plastic crib.

'D'you want t' hold her, then?' I ask him.

'*Hold her?*' he says. 'I dunno about that.' Hesitates. 'If I have to…'

I lean over to pick her up. He's stretching his arms out, awkward.

'Here you go, then,' I say, handing her to him.

He looks worried to death.

'Blimey,' he says, dead nervy, cradling her in his arms. 'She looks like me. Spitting image, don't you reckon?' Touches her foot. 'Feels ever so cold – is that all right? Normal?'

'They checked her just now,' I say. 'Said she was fine.'

Then, 'Look at her *fingers*,' he says. 'She's so *small*,' rubbing her palm with his thumb.

'I was so frightened,' I say.

'Don't tell me,' he says. 'Makes me feel sick – all that messy stuff. I don't want t' know.'

'I wish you could've been there…' I say.

She begins to cry and he tenses up.

'Here,' he says. 'You'd better have her,' and passes her back. Looks dead concerned. 'What's she crying for? What's up with her?'

I shrug.

'I s'pose she might want changing or feeding or something – I don't know. I'll ask, if she doesn't stop.'

But she seems to settle and he relaxes again.

'What we gunna call her, then?' I say.

'Nothin' fancy,' he says. 'I can't stand them fancy, poncy names.'

'But nothin' *too* ordinary,' I say. 'She's not an *ordinary* baby.'

'Can't we just call her Sprog or Small Kid? Keep it simple, like?'

'If you want...' I say – then tell her not to take any notice of him – because I don't.

I ask him if he can bring me a couple of things in; things I forgot and could do with. A bottle of Coke or something, and some shampoo.

'If I'm in a fit state,' he says. 'Out with the lads, later – celebrating.'

'Where you goin'?'

'Dunno. Everywhere, more than likely.'

'But you will come in, some time – later on?'

'Some time...'

'Have you sorted the room out – like we said?'

'Not yet. Give me a chance.'

'But you will get the cot off Tracey – move the bed and set it up in the corner...'

'I'll *do it*,' he says. 'If you give me a chance.'

I put the baby back in her crib.

Glance over at the couple next to us – you can hardly help it; they're both so gushy and excited. Touching each other and smiling like idiots. You won't catch Liam saying 'well done', or telling me how proud he is of me – not like this bloke to his wife. Liam's just *here*, and that's as much as I'll get from him. I'm past *wishing*...

We sit – me looking at him – him looking at the baby.

Then, 'Didn't want a boy, anyway,' he says. 'Boys get wrecked and fight all the time.'

But I can tell he's disappointed.

In a while, any talking dries up and I tell him I could use some rest now. Let him off the hook, before he does something, says something to spoil it all.

'See ya, then,' he says. 'Sleep tight,' and smiles as he dances off. And he does look proud, doesn't he? I tell meself, he just doesn't know what to say or how to say it, that's all.

I don't sleep much. Just lie there. Can't stop studying her. She's so beautiful. So amazing.

Every so often, I think I can't see her breathing and I have to poke her – make sure. Then she stirs and I wish I hadn't done it.

I don't want the nurses touching her. They can look, admire her – but I don't want them touching her. It's like I want to stand over and guard her. And I won't put her in the nursery either, even though they've suggested it – in case someone takes her, or she gets mixed up with another baby. This one's special. This one's *mine*.

I'm trying to think of her name. An important sounding name – not a kick-dirt-in-your-face name. I want her to feel important, because she is. I don't want her to feel how *I* feel. How I've always felt.

They say I'm getting on all right. Though the first time I change her it takes about half an hour. I don't know how to feed her. And as for bathing her – I don't think I'll tackle that, for a while, at least.

I don't know how to use sterilising fluid, how to tilt the crib, when to pick her up, when to leave her be.

Don't want to make meself look dim by asking daft questions.

I feel not good enough.

In the evening, Mum comes in, armed with a metallic silver balloon announcing 'It's a girl', attached to a fluffy pink rabbit.

'How're you feeling?' she says. 'Has she been good? Can I pick her up?' Wrapped up in it all, her questions don't require answers. 'Ahhh...She's just like you,' she drools. Lifting her out and holding her up, much to my irritation.

'Liam's been, I take it?'

'Yeh.'

'And...?'

'He's happy.'

'I should think so, too. Mind you, it must be a first,' launching into unintelligible ga–ga talk. Then carries on, 'She really is a little angel.'

She looks rough; her tight, stretchy jeans grubby. Her top bobbly and shapeless.

'Did you tell Dan?' I say.

'Did I tell Dan?! *Course!* I've told half the world. Everyone I've met!'

'What did he say?'

'Oh, you know men. They're not like us, don't get worked up about babies.' Thinks about it. 'Though he's pleased for you, of course. Didn't believe I'd been here all night, mind...'

'You look tired,' I say.

'What d'you expect? Didn't get any sleep!'

But it's more than tired. She's got a way about her that says something's wrong. And her eyes are too red.

'What d'you think of me hair?' she says.

It's yellow and stiff. Darker – orangey – at the roots.

'You've dyed it again,' I say. 'Thought Dan didn't like you bottle blonde.'

'So?' she says. 'He doesn't have to like it, does he? Nice though, innit? Reckon it makes me look a bit younger?'

77

When it starts to grow out, she'll look like a skunk.

'Yeh,' I say. 'A bit.'

I get embarrassed when Sarah and Mel turn up and Mum's still hanging around. Mum tries to join in, tries to be one of us. I wish she'd just be herself. I wish she didn't like Sarah's boots – want a pair. I wish she wasn't going *out on the raz* tonight with her mates. And I wish she didn't paint her nails screaming blue.

Me, Sarah and Mel – we don't talk the same with Mum around.

'She's a really cute baby,' Mel says.

'She's *god-damn-gorgeous*,' Mum says.

'What was it like, Lise,' Sarah says, 'was it awful?'

'She was fine,' Mum says. 'Just fine.'

When I can get a word in edgeways, we end up chatting politely about how nice, how comfortable, hospitals are these days. How friendly the staff are and how you get – as Mum puts it – all mod cons. But I really don't want to talk – not to any of them – bar showing me baby off, I admit.

'How long they keeping you?' Sarah asks.

''Bout five days...'

'Enjoy it while you can,' Mum says. ''Cause then it's out into the big, wide world; that's when reality'll kick in.'

I'm glad when they go.

I sit there. Watching, getting to know my baby. Our baby. Though, in a way, I feel like I've always known her.

Spend the rest of the evening just doing that. And missing me gran like crazy.

When Liam shows up, the following morning, reality is something he wants nothing to do with. He's late, hung over and fast getting hacked off.

'Give me a *break*,' he says. 'I don't *know* when we'll be able to get a flat. Or even *if* we'll be able to.'

'It's gunna be really difficult at Evelyn's,' I say. 'You said so yourself. And we've got some money together now.'

'We?' he says. 'Don't you mean *I've* got some money together?'

'What's that supposed to mean?'

'Nothing,' he says. 'Nothing. Just change the record; it's all I ever hear about.'

Liam doesn't like the name Alexandra. Alexandra Lucy. Thinks it's too posh; nobby. I try and tempt him, 'But Alex – that's not posh, is it? That's what she'd be called by everyone.'

'What's wrong with Kelly?' he says. 'I like Kelly.'

Whatever I want, is wrong. Whatever I say, is wrong.

And every time I give in, I give something of meself away; it's like I just don't matter.

'You didn't bring me that stuff, last night...'

'Didn't have time. Here...' he says.

He's brought the Coke I asked for – though only a can, and has forgotten the shampoo. Takes it from his jacket pocket and puts it on the bedside table, next to the whiffy, speckled bananas and half pound of green grapes that Mel brought.

'What about... Isabella?' I say.

'What about The Duchess of York?' he says, sarcastic.

'All right then,' I say. 'We'll call her The Duchess of York.'

'*Kelly*,' he says.

'Kelly, Duchess of York?'

'If you like,' he says. 'It's better than *Alexandra*,' putting on a voice, 'or *Is-a-bloody-bella*.'

'I was only winding you up with *Isabella*...' I say. Then, 'Remember that girl up the arcades? *Araminta*?'

'Out of it, she was,' he says. 'Blasted.'

'But she was all right, though. I felt sorry for her.'

'Head–case,' he says. 'Her old man a bloody barrister as well...What a laugh.'

'We had some fun though, didn't we?' I say.

He sort of smiles.

'Yeh, we had a crack.'

'Last summer – that was the best summer I've ever had in me whole life.'

'It was all right...'

''Member when...'

'Everything okay?' The nurse butts in, in passing. 'How's *Dad*?'

He cringes, sinking into the chair.

'All right,' he mumbles.

'Coping?' She grins.

'It's all right,' he says.

I wish she'd get lost; I cut her dead and lower me voice. ''Member when we went fishing in the river that night – when we all piled back to Sarah's soaked through?'

'Her old dear,' he says, 'did she ever freak, or what?'

But the silence that follows is uneasy.

He's looking around the ward.

'See him – over there,' he says. 'Prat – keeps looking at us.'

'P'raps he's jealous,' I say. ''Cause we're young and gorgeous.'

'He's a *prat*,' he says, aggressive.

They're talking about us, opposite. I can tell. Talking and sneering.

'Shouldn't worry about it,' I say. '*You'll* be forty with a droopy moustache and an anorak, one day.'

'No way,' he says. 'No way will I ever be an anorak. Or have a droopy *anything*.'

'Can't imagine them *doing it*, can you?'

'I'd rather not. Mind you, I can't imagine us *doing it* again, either.'

'Don't be daft,' I say. 'We'll be all right. When we get out, get a flat…'

'Here we go again…' he says.

Evelyn turns up.

'A flying visit. Thought I'd better show me face. Why aren't you working, young man?' she asks.

'Got time off…'

'Skiving, more like,' she says. 'You can't afford t' miss too many days. I've been meaning to say – about your keep – you're gunna have to give me a bit more. I can't run that house on pennies alone for much longer…'

'How *much* more?' he says.

'I'll have to work it out…but what I'm getting off you at the minute doesn't cover anything; you're gunna have to put your hand in your pocket; fork out.'

'There's nothin' in me pocket!'

'Dig a bit deeper…' she says. Then, to me, 'Anything you need?'

'Shampoo,' I say.

'Shampoo?' she sniggers. 'Give it a couple days and you won't have time to worry about *yourself*. You'll be up to your neck…' Then comes the advice. 'Mind you slap plenty of zinc and castor on her behind, if you don't want her getting sore,' and, looking into the crib, 'They always used to say to lay them on their front. I always found…'

'They said, put her on her back.'

'Yeh, well, that's all right – but what if she's sicky – chokes?'

'They said, she won't. That she's best off on her back – it's safer.'

She raises her eyebrows and pulls a face.

'They tell you all sorts,' she says. 'But most of 'em have never had one of their own – and there's no substitute for *experience*.'

Luckily, she sticks to her word; is in and out quite quickly. I'm glad to see the back of her, before the baby starts to stir.

Her little hands going up and a heavy frown coming across her face, before she cries out – wah, wah, wah…!

I ask Liam if he wants to pick her up; hold her. Try and settle her.

'You can do it,' he says. 'I held her yesterday.'

Nine

One way or another, I'm gunna get this baby lark right.

I'm definitely learning – fast – how to be a mum. She scares me sometimes. But I *know* I can care for her well. And there's one thing for certain – I'll always be around, when it matters.

I feel so protective of her, it's weird. Protective, but not protected.

It's different to how I feel about Liam. What I feel about him is something that changes; is changing.

Evelyn says, 'Fact number one – you should always put your man first.'

But then, Evelyn talks out of her arse.

Anyway, I'm sick to death of people telling me what I should and shouldn't do. Why don't they take a look at their own lives instead of mine? I mean, I'm not a bleedin' disaster area. I know it won't be easy. But I love my baby enough to get through. And she'll love me back, I can feel it, already. She really *needs* me. And I don't care what anyone else thinks.

Mum's one of the worst culprits. Coming in again, brimming with important little lessons to be learnt – 'Mind you wind her properly after she's fed' – all that guff. And later on, wouldn't you know it, Evelyn's back.

I ask her, where's Liam been. I'm due home tomorrow; didn't see him at all yesterday – and there's no sign, so far, today.

'Working,' she says. 'He can't keep missing days.'

'It's not days… It's half an hour – before he starts, or when he's finished.'

'You've only had a baby,' she says. 'You're not dying.'

'He wasn't working last night, though,' I say.

'Don't involve me,' she says, involving herself. 'He had a hard day. Needed some time to himself.'

'Luxury…' I say.

'Necessity,' she says.

'Fat chance – from now on,' I say, making something of it, just for the hell of it – and because I feel let down.

'It was your decision…' she says.

I glare at her.

'*Our* decision. And we won't regret it.'

She smirks.

'Don't kid yourself. This is all very hard for Liam,' she says. 'I don't know how you think you're gunna manage.

'We'll be all right.'

'I've been talking to him,' she says. 'He's really het up. Got himself into a right old tiz.'

'What's he said, then?'

'It's not for me to interfere,' she says. 'After all, you're two grown-up people – or so you think,' loosening her chiffon scarf, touching her earrings. 'But something's got t' give. Soon.'

'What...?'

'I wonder,' she says, clearing her smoky throat, 'if you couldn't go and stay with your mum, for a while.'

'Why? What for?'

'It just might be a good idea – till you're sorted.'

'Is that what Liam said?'

'We talked about it...' she says.

'But is that what *he said*?'

'Just think about it,' she says. 'That's all I'm saying. It's not such a bad idea, y'know. See how things go...'

'I want him to come in,' I say. 'I want to talk to him.'

'He can't just drop everything, day after day...'

'*I want to see him.*'

'Don't push him,' she says. 'It'll only make things worse.'

'*Push him?*' I say. 'What're you on about?'

She sighs. Picks up her bag.

'I'm nipping out for a fag. I won't be long. Just think about it, eh?'

Teeters off in her cheap, clicky slingbacks and pencil pleat skirt. Cow. Bag.

There's no way I'm going to Mum and Dan's. I mean – why? It's ridiculous. It's unthinkable. And it's not gunna happen.

And like – what about Mum? Has she *asked* her? Have they been having cosy little chit chats, or something? In private? Discussing *me*? *My* life? Poring over the possibilities? They *can't* have. Mum would've blacked her eye, for a start. And still might, yet, if she's not careful.

All the time she's gone, I'm getting madder and madder; steaming.

She's gone for ages. Maybe she's not coming back...? Just thought she'd stir things up a bit, then leg it.

Some clown from hospital radio comes along.

'Any requests...?' he says.

'Yeh. Sod off and leave me alone.'

Looks mystified. Disappears fast.

I'm watching the others, angry, as they drool and drone.

'Have you got Lionel Richie and Diana Ross – "Endless Love"?'

For God's sake.

I hate them for how they seem to get all the attention. All the affection; anything they want. For all their silky robes and neat hair and wedding rings. Their lipsticked mouths and their attitude.

Any confidence I'd started to feel is slipping away. Wiped away, by just a few words and looks.

Without any warning, I start to cry. Not just wimpy weeping, either. Not polite crying; a few sniffles into a scrap of white lace. More like gibbering idiot crying, bawling into a kacky old nightie.

'I've brought you a coffee, love,' the nurse says. 'Thought you could use one.' Then, 'D'you want a chat? D'you want to talk about anything?' Putting the plastic cup down beside me.

'They often get emotional, a few days after the birth,' she says to Evelyn, who's waltzed back in. 'But we'll look after her.' Draws the curtain round to stop the happy-crew from gawping. Tells her they'll keep an eye on me – have a word with the doctor, if needs be. 'She'll be all right.'

Evelyn says, quietly, 'Come on. Don't make a spectacle of yourself. Calm down.'

'Just *go*,' I say. But she won't; sits there.

'See what I mean, though?' she says.

'*What?*'

'You – getting in a state and all. It's not going to be so easy, is it?'

'I *won't* go to Mum's,' I say.

'Nothing t' do with *me*, love,' she says. 'It's Liam who…'

'*What?*'

She takes a breath. Hesitates.

'*He* suggested it. Not me…' she says. 'Just give him some *space*. He feels *trapped*. Like *you've* trapped him.' Then, 'Don't you see – I can't have you back to my place – he is my son, after all. And he needs some time – if you're gunna stand any chance…Just for a while, eh?'

Part Three

Part Three

Ten

It seems like my whole life is controlled by other people. Without Mum, I wouldn't even have a place to live.

I didn't come quietly. But although I'd like to say that I ripped into Liam – gave him a proper pasting – I can't, because I haven't seen him yet, not set eyes on him. I came because I had no choice.

Mum got really organised in no time – racing around like a blue-arsed fly, she was; cot collected and banged together, room upside down and sorted, bits and pieces bought from here and there. Loose mouths firmly shut. (To Evelyn – 'If you say "give the boy some time" just *once* more…How much time does the little bleeder need? A week? A month? A bloody lifetime?' *Right* in her face.)

Dan said, 'I don't give a damn who comes here to stay – *I* won't be around for long.'

And Mum said, 'It's nothing t' do with you – and I don't give a damn whether you give a damn,' sticking her middle finger up and poking her tongue out. That's what she told me, anyhow.

He's told Mum he wants out; they're splitting up. Decided a while ago but it's taken a bit of time for him to get it sorted – get himself another place.

Mum's staying here, in the house. He says, she's welcome; it's crap. Turned out, it's not *Dan's* place, like he first had her believe – it's rented. Not that she can afford to pay the rent; can't even manage *half* of it.

'What'll you do?' I say.

'What *can I do*?' she says.

I hate the way he's made a fool of her; never really wanting her at all. Just playing.

She's putting a hard face on it. I'm going easy on her; I know what it's like to feel used, like you're less than nothing.

But I'm here with her, for now, at least. Knackered, but here.

Y'know somebody told me once, back along, that all babies really do for the first nine months of their lives, is eat, leak and *sleep*.

Well, it's lies, lies, lies! *Mountains of guff.*

Let me tell you – babies only ever *pretend* to sleep. In the stillness of the early hours, or whenever, makes no difference. When you're done in, dead beat, exhausted. They pretend they're going to let you rest. Even let you nod off for ten minutes. Then they're away –

WAH, WAH, WAH! All through the night and most of the day, it seems.

'Can't you shut that kid up?' Dan hollers. 'I can't stand it much more.'

Well, sometimes I can quieten her – and sometimes I can't. I'm doing me best, for God's sake. Wah, wah, wah!

But he won't have to *stand it* much more, will he?

Mum loves Alex, she does. Loves her to bits.

And my baby's still beautiful. When I take time to really look at her, properly. But I'm too tired to notice much these days. Tireder than I've ever known or thought possible.

Even so, I still wish – sometimes – that Mum wouldn't breeze in and take over. I know she intends well, but it makes me feel so useless. Useless – and *in the way* – what with Dan and all that. It's really awkward, but, like I said, I didn't have another option. Like a smack in the face, it was. Only worse.

Dan's packing up his hi-fi just now. Pulling the leads out, coiling them up. Chucking them in a box.

'Don't electrocute yourself, will you?' Mum sneers as she passes.

'Don't worry, I'm not as thick as you,' he says, cool. Carefully lifting each piece and then stacking CDs and tapes alongside.

Then Alex starts again, wah, wah, wah!

'Stick somethin' in that youngan's gob,' he says, bored and impatient. As if it was that simple.

She won't feed properly. I couldn't feed her meself, and now she's fighting against the bottle. Pushing the teat out with her tongue and getting right worked up.

'Let me try,' Mum says. 'Give her here,' holding out her arms.

'It's all right, she'll settle down…'

'Give her here,' she says. 'I have done this before, y'know.'

And all the time, Dan's huffing away in the background.

'Nightmare,' he says. 'Bloody nightmare,' as Mum whisks Alex through to the kitchen. Then, 'She's not so perfect, y'know – your mother,' he says to me. 'Some of the things I could tell you about her…'

I go on upstairs, out of the way. Flop down on the bed and try not to cry so much that they'll be able to tell from me eyes. Can't put up with his hormones and waterworks jibes. Or her concern, making it even worse.

All I really want, is to be left alone, with Alex. But then, I don't know if I could do it – by meself.

Keep thinking – if Liam was different…I really thought I knew him, to start off with. I thought we were the same. A pair. That we'd be all right, somehow.

In a while, Mum brings Alex up to the bedroom.

'She's done and dusted; changed and all.'

Puts her down, carefully, into the rickety cot. 'If she seems too warm, take that top cover off…'

'I *know*…'

'I'm just saying,' she says. 'Only trying t' help. And don't forget – the health visitor's due t' sniff around later. Don't go giving her anythin' t' gripe about, any ammunition – 'cause once they've got hold of you…' Then, 'What time's Lord Liam meant t' be coming?'

I shrug, insides twisting at the thought.

Dead nervous about seeing him. Had a belly ache all day. Ever since Evelyn phoned.

''Bout three, I think.'

'Finishing work early, then?'

'How do I know?'

94

She looks stern, flicks her hair around a bit.

'I'll make meself scarce when he gets here. Might say too much, otherwise.' Just stands there, waiting for me to respond.

'When's Dan going?' I ask.

'Not soon enough,' she snaps. Then, 'Hasn't said, exactly; later on, as far as I'm aware.'

The health visitor cancels. Makes no odds; she's useless, anyway. Seems to want to know everything but do nothing. Says she'll come Friday, instead.

I've got more important things to think about.

The last time I saw Liam was in the hospital, over three weeks ago, now. Haven't stopped thinking about it, about him. Turning it over and over in me head.

One minute, I hate him. All angry and torn up, I want to fight him. The next, I don't know how I feel. Confusion. Hope, mingled with bitterness. Like, if he walked in today – said sorry – said let's start over – let's give it a go…

Then I wonder, is it him, or me? Is there something about *me* that makes people push me away? First, there was Dad. Then Mum, when she found Dan. Now Liam.

I've got to stay calm when he comes. Give him a chance, or he'll just up and leave. In which case I'd never know – how it might have been. Could've been.

Five to three comes and Mum slams the door hard behind herself. I curse her for it; for waking Alex. She probably would've gone another half hour, given me and Liam time on our own, but instead it's wah, wah, wah! Again. The tune that's etched on my brain.

I cradle her against me. Waiting. Shaking. Waiting. I feel

sorry for her. She deserves better than I fear she's going to get. Helpless in this mess.

When I think of what other babies, other children have – the snooty cows' in the hospital – it makes me sick. *I* want something good for *my* baby, too. She's just as special. Just as important. But all she's got is me. Nothing fancy, no frills, me. Doesn't seem a whole lot, right now. That's why I've got to keep strong – for her. What *I* want and feel and need isn't so important any more; it's all about her, now.

My stomach gives a hard turn, when Dan lets Liam in.

He's late and full of himself. I strain to hear them, catch what they're saying, all matey and laddish, though they hardly know one another. Something about the rain, the clutter…something about the football.

I've changed Alex into a little suit that Mel gave me. Looks as good as new. Soft blue leggings and a fire engine top. Navy socks with lime hoops and a little hat. She looks smart and clean and cute. It's one of the best things she's got.

I feel ill; ache, as he comes up the stairs.

Got to stay calm; got to stay calm.

'Looks like an old man,' is his opening shot, as he walks in, sees her. Laughing at her, his voice light, though clumsy, a bit nervy.

'I think she looks lovely,' I say, hurt.

'I wouldn't take her down the pub like it…' somehow trying to joke.

'She's not going down the pub, is she?' I say. 'But I'd be proud to take her *anywhere.*'

'Keep your hair on,' he says. 'I didn't mean…Look, shall I go out and come back in; start again?'

'Why don't you?' I say, giving him a 'Gran' look.

And he does, literally. Putting on a voice now.

'Oh, hello there, how're you today?' All cardboard and kiddish, starting to irritate me already. I ignore it. Deep breath, then:

'Everyone says she's doing well,' I say. He looks at her. 'If you're interested?' I add.

'Course I'm *interested*.' Parking his bum against the radiator. Turning his glance to the window and beyond. He doesn't *look* interested.

'See that?' he says, nodding outside.

'What?' I say.

'The Mean Machine.'

Standing outside is a beat-up bike, a heap and a half.

'Whose is that?'

'Mine, stupid. It don't look much, but it's a 350cc. Like it?' Then, 'Great to have transport.'

I hate it; it's crap and a waste of money.

I wonder how much he paid for it, but don't ask. Don't want t' know. I don't praise it up, obviously – but I don't freak, either. God – it's hard; keepin' me mouth shut when there's so much I could say. Don't know how long I can keep it up. I'm so *angry*.

We start to chat – about rubbish that doesn't matter, about nothing – but it doesn't get any easier. Any more normal.

Though I do keep a watch on me sharpness, and after a bit, he seems to lose his cockiness.

Then, when I think it's all right, safe –

'Are you really interested?' I say.

There's quiet.

'I'm here, aren't I?'

97

I don't know what to say to him. *Mustn't be sarcastic;
mustn't wind him up.*

I want to belt him one.

I want him to want me.

I pick Alex up; she's grizzling.

'She's a really good baby,' I tell him.

'Yeh?'

I nod.

'Want to hold her?'

He's all arms and awkward. Reluctant.

'She won't eat your head,' I say, handing her over.

'But she's so weeny,' he says, dead uncomfortable.

'She's grown loads,' I tell him.

'Is this right, how I've got hold of her?' he says. 'I don't
want to hurt her.'

'She's a tough nut, like me,' I say. 'You won't hurt her.'

Scared that he will hurt her – in time – if he doesn't
love her enough. If he doesn't care enough.

We sit there for a while.

'So…' I say.

'So what?' he says, eventually.

'So – what're we going to do?'

'How d'you mean?' he says, looking both blank and
guilty as hell. Then, 'Well. I thought…' he starts, trailing
off to nothing.

'You thought what?'

'I dunno…'

'What were you going to say?'

'Well. I thought we'd…just see how it goes.'

I don't want to *see how it goes.* I want to scream at
him…I want to lay into him…I want to punch the
living daylights out of him.

I want him to want us and I want him to finish what he's started.

But I hold it all in. In some vague and pathetic hope that he'll change his mind; grow up.

Then, 'Saw the old gang, last night,' he pipes up, changing the subject but still uptight.

'Yeh?' I say, dead flat.

He carries on, 'Yeh. Still the same crack – bit of a laugh and all that.'

'Oh…'

'Still ripping the mick out of everybody…larking about. Nothin's changed, like.'

'No?' I say, dry. 'Not for that lot, maybe.'

He almost looks embarrassed, but not quite.

'I told them all about her,' he says, nodding towards Alex.

'Told them what? You don't know anything about her.'

He's annoyed. In a matter-of-fact way, says, 'Look – if you didn't want me to come…'

I can't back off.

'I need to know some things,' I say. 'Like – what's going to happen; when you're going to see her – all that stuff. If you even *want* to see her…'

'Course I do,' he says.

'And I need to know about *us*. If there still is an *us*…'

'I told you,' he says. 'Let's just see how it goes, eh? We don't need it all *mapped out*, do we? I don't need t' make an *appointment* to come round here, do I?'

'No – but I'd like an *idea*…And what about money?' I say. 'It's not fair on Mum…'

'Ah, *money*,' he goes. 'Funny how everything seems to come down to money in the end.'

99

'Well, at least tell me,' I say. 'Whether we're together, or apart.'

He lays Alex back in the cot, still stiff and uneasy with her. As if he hasn't heard what I said. Gives her the dummy but doesn't pull the blanket up. Then, eventually, 'We're together *and* apart,' he says.

'What's that s'posed to mean?'

'What I said...'

'Well, what did you tell your little *gang* about us? About *me*?' I say.

'Nothing. We didn't talk about *you*,' he says.

They all seem so childish now, from where I'm standing. Like, all of a sudden, we're *miles* apart.

I know it's all over.

'Lisa and Liam' just doesn't feel right any more. Doesn't fit. Doesn't even *sound* right. Sounds...pathetic.

Eleven

Everyone says I'm coping, so I s'pose I must be.

'You're doing all right,' they say. 'Really well.'
Patronising; meaning – *all things considered... Under the circumstances...*

I guess, then, it's normal that the baby does nothing but cry; that I do nothing but cry. Shut away, on me own; secretly.

I want someone to help me, but at the same time, I don't – I have to be able to manage myself. And I'm determined to show them – I'm not just some kid who's messed up – I *can* do it.

Tho' sometimes, it's like I live in this imaginary world. I can't stop it – making up stories, fantasies in me mind – about how sorry Liam'll be. How, one day, he'll turn up on the doorstep – saying he's made a big mistake – begging me to go back to him. To some nice place he's gone all out to find us. Some place with squashy sofas, thick creamy carpets and oil paintings on the walls. And I'll take a look at it and say '...No thanks. Stuff it. I've got something better; *someone* better.' Waltz out on him.

Though in reality, I still want him. But like I thought he was, not how he is. I thought – at first – he was on my side. That's what I wanted to believe.

He never calls. He never comes. He said he'd come, but he doesn't. And all these scenes, these dreams – of the good Liam – fester away; driving me nuts...Liam with another girl...Liam with another girl who's all pretty and poncified...Liam with another girl and their baby...Liam happy. I don't want him to be happy. I want him to hurt. I want to hurt him. Want him to really *feel it*, like I do.

Alex stops me from going mad but drives me insane. Needing something, all the time. There's no let up. Needing *me*. And they're all waiting for me to slip up. Step in – and tell me *how to do it properly*.

It feels like the old me – the lippy, gobby me – has faded away. *I'm* fading away.

I don't say anything – stick up for meself – when I should. I'm angry for letting them make me feel like this – but I'm not up to a row. I'd just start bawling again like some soft-as-shit failure, and they'd all go, 'I knew it...She can't cope...it was inevitable.' Gloating experts, everywhere.

It's not just Alex crying that gets me down. There's feeding, bathing, changing, washing, drying, ironing, shopping; no money, no time, no space, no sleep.

Though it's funny – that even though I want to rest, the special times always seem to be at night. When me and Alex are on our own, away from them all. And I'm watching her, and she's looking up at me... That's when I think I can win. I *will* win. That I've got no regrets – and her needing me is a comfort.

It must've been really hard for Mum – when she had me young; no one helped her. No one.

It's really hard for her *now*. I give her as much as I can – out of what I get from the Social – but it's not a lot. Not enough.

'Don't worry,' she says. 'We'll manage somehow.'

I'm trying not to judge her so much, these days. Even so, I'd never let Alex down – like Mum let me down when Dan came along. Not for Liam, not for anyone.

Then I hear – that Liam seems to be managing, very nicely. Might be going away – with the others – so Sarah reckons.

'Remember – we said about it? Grape picking or somethin' like that. But don't worry, I'll keep an eye on him for you.'

'Don't bother,' I say. 'Makes no odds to me,' putting a face on it. Lying.

She looks awkward.

'Well,' she says. 'I don't s'pose you can blame him for wanting...' eats her words.

'For wanting what? To get away?' I snap. 'Can't I? Why not?'

'I didn't mean...I mean, for wanting to get out of this dump – not for wanting to leave you and...'

'I know what you meant...' I say, giving Alex a little kiss as she nuzzles in to me.

Sarah hesitates.

'There's nothing for us lot, here, is there?' she says. 'I mean, no decent jobs and that…'

'He's not the only one short on lolly and laughs…'

Then, she back-pedals, 'Well. He might not come, yet.'

I shrug. 'Like I said, makes no odds to me.'

'He's really proud of Alex,' she says.

'Yeh?' I say, not taken in.

'Yeh. He doesn't talk about her much – but when he does, says it's good, being a dad.'

I'm sick of this conversation. She's got no idea.

Goes on about the new gear she got down the market – about what she's getting next week – some fancy pair of trainers. Only *twelve ninety-nine*. I'm just not interested.

'You ought t' come down,' she says. 'Have a look. You haven't got anything new for ages, have you?'

'Not fussed.'

'Go on,' she says. Then, all excited, 'I'm gunna get me belly button pierced too – week after next; why don't you have it done with me…? Be a laugh…'

'Oh *yeh*. They wouldn't be able to find me belly button.'

'Rubbish,' she says. 'You've lost your baby weight now; most of it, anyhow. Your *legs* look skinny.'

'Not me *legs* they'd be punching a hole in and hanging a ring on, is it?' I don't go so far as to *show* her the whale blubber hiding under me jumper; making me feel like a freak with six stomachs – all of them made of jelly. But I can't be arsed to think about it, let alone talk about it, *do something* about it. Still slobbed out in the same tracky bottoms and top I've been in for…ever, it feels. Nice milky marks on the shoulders. She smells of *Charlie Gold*', I smell of formula baby milk and sick.

'You ought to come out one night,' she says. 'Up the arcades, like we used to.'

It seems like another lifetime; on another planet.

'Might do,' I say, knowing I won't.

'Go on,' she says, 'do you good – to get out.'

Which makes me feel even worse, like she feels *so sorry* for me; she doesn't really *want* me to come – I'm a charity case.

'I don't like leaving Alex...'

'Why not? She'll be all right with your mum, won't she?'

'S'pose,' I say. But in truth I feel funny about it. Don't like being away from her – in case something happens to her, while I'm not here.

'Or bring her.'

'Bring her?'

'Yeh. She'll be okay. For an hour. And everyone can see her.'

The thought of *that lot*, pawing her, mauling her...

'Maybe...' Like maybe, never.

Turns out, I can't avoid them. Not for the want of trying.

Walking through the playground – feeling a right nerd, I am, what with the pushchair; I'm still not used to it.

'Lisa! Over here!' The little gang, huddled behind the shelter. Looking small and acting big, as ever.

'All right?' I say.

'Where've you been? We don't see you no more...'

I look down at Alex.

'Where d'you think?'

They all gawp, ooh and ahh for a minute – say she's cute, say she's this, she's that.

Then, 'Got any fags…?'

'Got any cash on you…?'

'Boring, innit?'

Liam is leaning against the fence. He's in a black leather bomber jacket that I've not seen before; is looking dead cool – and will just be *dead* if he doesn't speak.

'All right?'

'All right.'

Comes over and bends down, putting on a show for the crowd.

'How's my girl? Mummy looking after you?'

I ought to smack him one.

'She's perfect,' I say. 'She's just perfect.'

Stands up again.

Takes a cigarette out and lights up. Steps back to his place on the fence. Moving further along, as I get closer; leaving the others jabbering on about some rubbish; novelty passed.

'You're going away, then?' I say.

He shrugs his shoulders, still walking, slowly.

'Dunno. P'raps.'

'That's what I heard.'

'You don't want t' believe everything you hear.'

'I don't. I'm just saying.'

'P'raps,' he says again. 'I might do. Have to see.'

He won't look at me any more. Stares beyond me. Taking deep drags and blowing the smoke straight out, as if he doesn't know how to inhale properly. Edgy, in case I'm about to show him up in front of his mates.

'They're after me for money,' he says.

'Who?'

'The government – who d'you think?'

'Oh…'

'You put 'em on t' me, I s'pose?'

'You are working – you could give us *something*.'

'It's not like I'm a millionaire, though, is it? Sent me this bloody form – want t' know the ins and outs of a cat's arse.'

'Have you sent it back?'

'Have I hell! Must be joking. I binned it. It's all I get, lately – hassle.'

'You can't just *dump us*,' I say.

'I *haven't*.'

'Then why haven't we seen you?'

'I've been busy.'

'You could at least try.'

'I have, but…'

'*Try harder*, then.'

'What you saying – I'm not good enough, right?'

'No – I'm not saying you're not good enough. I'm saying – you don't even exist, any more.'

'Crap. Just 'cause I haven't seen her *lately*. But at least I don't give you a hard time; give you grief.'

'*What?* I don't believe you just *said* that.'

'All I'm saying is – it could be worse. You want a fairy tale – this is real life.' Then, 'I *need* t' get away,' he says.

'So you'll go away – and blame us?' I say.

'No. I'll go away, 'cause I *want* to.'

'She's your baby, too,' I say.

'*I know*,' he snaps back. 'But I didn't ask you t' get pregnant, did I?'

'No,' I say. 'And she didn't ask to be born.'

'Listen…' he starts.

'No, Liam, *you* listen,' I say. 'Face it. You're just one hell of a *wanker*.'

Sarah bounds over.

'Ahh, look at her... Lovely, in't she?'

I turn me back on them. Nobody seems to notice much as we leave. Nobody's bothered, beyond a 'see ya' and a glance.

Town passes me by – a cloud of thoughts and feelings jamming up me head. The usual – what he said – what I said – what I *should've* said – how I *should've* floored him – all dancing around, becoming no clearer.

Inside the home is airy, but still somehow heavy and close. Tatty, except for a few nice plants dotted around the place.

A stiff, padded chair sits by the grey, unlit gas fire, hanging on the wall.

'Who's this coming, now?' a crotchety, slurred voice says. I try and smile.

'Hello, Gran,' I say.

She looks at me, at the pushchair.

'Whose kiddy is that?'

'Mine. You remember – Mum told you.'

'You know your trouble?' she says.

'What's that?' I say.

'You're a *liar* – that's what. Always have been, always will be.' Then, 'What's happened to the stuff you said you'd bring me?'

'What stuff?'

'You *know*,' she says. 'What you said...'

I don't know what she's on about, and neither does she.

108

Turns her head towards the wall, dazzly papered; pukey pink floral.

I wheel the buggy to the side, out of the way. Tuck the blanket in and stroke Alex on the cheek; all smiley, she is. Pull up a stool and perch on it, uncomfortable – me legs not fitting into the space.

'They're all bone idle, in here,' she mutters to herself. 'Bone bloody idle.'

Her hair is stuck flat to her head. She's still wearing those damn beads – brash and bold. Her eyelids look weighted down with tiredness. Years of tiredness.

Gradually, her breathing slows and her head drops down as she nods off. Lets out a little moan, like a cry.

'All right, Gran?' I whisper. 'It's all right…'

I sit, watching her.

Feeling guilty – for all our arguments and fights. We had plenty – though I don't suppose it matters now.

I sit, just watching.

And when she's sound asleep, she becomes the old Gran. Bull-headed and stubborn, but with all the answers and ways out.

What would she tell me? What would she say?

She'd shift about, sucking on her wet-ended fag. Shoulders back, pretending to be narky – but enjoying being the boss.

'Forget him,' she'd say. 'If you need a clown in your life – visit the bloody circus. It's more fun and cheaper in the long run.' Another hard suck on the fag. She'd tell me – he doesn't care about me, he doesn't want me, and he'll never respect me. He's got no feelings, he's got no brains and he's got no *right*. So there. She'd tell me to sit tight, for now. After all, you never know what's round the corner. And she'd tell me to think about what I've got. What *he's* lost. To look forwards – not back.

I look at Alex, lying there, peaceful. Beautiful. Hopeful.

'Come on, girl,' she'd say. '*Don't be a fool.* Show 'em – you can do it; *you can do it damn well.*'

I lean over, touch her face. Pull back.

She was never a touchy, huggy gran – she wouldn't want me to touch her now. She didn't go in for soft words, either; don't be daft, she'd say, cross. But I whisper, anyway.

'Thanks, Gran...'

Part Four

Part Four

Twelve

Me and Mel are sat in the café, sharing a plate of cakes over the two kids.

'Is it like you imagined,' she asks, ' – this whole baby thing?'

I shrug.

'S'pose not.'

'Not as... *fluffy* as you thought?'

'I never thought it was gunna be fluffy,' I say. 'I knew it'd be hard.'

'Getting better, though?'

'Yeh...'

'What about Liam?' she asks.

'Who?' I say.

She smiles.

'Well done!' Then quietly, 'You've got guts.'

Talks about her 'sometimes bloke' – how he waltzes in,

'...filling the room with his sweaty trainers, his ego and – hark,' she says, putting her hand to her ear, 'is that the babbling stream of bullshit I hear?' And we have a giggle.

'Dump him,' I say.

'Yeh, well. Maybe...' Then, with a mixture of experience and disgust, 'What does Liam look like first thing in the morning?' she says. 'Don't tell me – a flabby arse and a creased up face, I'll bet?'

'Yep.'

'I *knew* it,' and we both laugh.

She's brushing sugar – fresh from a jam doughnut – off her jumper. Catches sight of the pair of us in the mirror.

'Look at me,' she says, eyes all clear and tigerish. 'Thought me body'd be shot to pieces after giving birth – but I'm bloody *gorgeous*!'

I run me fingers through me hair.

'I'm not s' bad meself...'

'Not bad at all,' she says. ''Cept for the incontinence, of course!'

'Thanks, Mel, you're a real pal!'

'Cheers!' she says, and we both gulp the hot, sweet tea.

When I get home, the house smells lovely. Of bum cream and powder and clean washing.

'Used to stink of wet dog and veg,' Mum says. 'So things are definitely looking up.'

Alex is sleeping. I leave the pram in the corner, go and sit down on me own, in the quiet.

I'm thinking – first about Gran. And about how I can't do anything, say anything to make it better for her.

Then, about Mum – the years of me and her, together in our flat. Happier with me mind wandering.

Remembering…the details of our lives that don't sound important, but that somehow bring a rush of feelings to the surface. Good feelings.

Thinking of when I was little; sorting through her box of yellowy jewels – believing that every crystallish glimmer was a real diamond, set in real gold. Remembering – the painting on the wall in the front room – the one Mum bought, but used to tell people she'd done herself. And the bubbly Mr Matey baths together on a Sunday night.

Short skirts, long skirts, *Top of the Pops* on the telly, dancing away, before bed on a Thursday. Waggon Wheel biscuits and packet ham. Beef paste on sliced bread, followed by minty Matchmaker chocolates. How she used to get cross with me for lying upside down on the settee; and for walking backwards along the road when she sent me out for twenty Silk Cut and ten Anadin. How she always said she wanted to be like Tina Turner, pouting her lips out, caked with pink. How she never let things get to her; never gave up.

Then Mum comes in. Brushes my arm with her hand.

'All right, love?'

'Fine,' I say.

'Yeh,' she says, sighing. 'I think we're getting there, aren't we?'

I peek at Alex, warm and safe.

'Yeh,' I say, 'we're getting there.'

Also of interest:

Sandra Chick
On the Rocks

'My mother isn't eating. She very seldom does. She's
leaning against the wall, head to one side, the way she
holds herself when she's flirting. My father isn't eating
either. Too busy watching her. Unimpressed. "Still
standing, dear?" he says.'

Jinny wishes she had a mum she could admire and be close to.
Instead, she spends her time worrying about whether Mum's
going to get drunk again and do something daft — or dangerous.
Then, one day, her mum really does overdo it and ends up in
hospital. Her dad's no help, her older sister Kate's given up, and
Alice, the baby, is just too young to understand. It looks like the
whole family is on the rocks. But Jinny's determined to survive . . .

'Outstanding.' *Vogue*

Fiction £3.99
ISBN 0 7043 4938 8

Sandra Chick
Cheap Street

'When we part, it's with few words that don't mean
anything. See you soon, take care, and all that rubbish. I
walk home the long way. Avoiding the places I've seen
Kelly's sister hanging out, on account I don't want my
face smashed in. Stand on the bridge. Looking back
towards home. Wondering – when I'll see me mum again.
Feeling beaten up and angry inside.'

Somewhere between the labour ward and the benefit office, Lisa
Brunt's mother lost her spark. Lisa's determined that won't
happen to her. But how do you carve out a life for yourself if
you're stuck on a run-down housing estate, your clothes are
scruffy, you're not skinny enough, and your mum's gone off with
Dan the Man? Lisa takes it day by day, surrounded by cheap food,
cheap clothes, cheap fags, cheap living, as she looks for a way off
Cheap Street . . .

'Utterly believable and very compelling.' *The Times*

Fiction £4.99
ISBN 0 7043 4949 3

Sandra Chick

I Never Told Her I Loved Her

**"'You'll miss me one day," Mum had said.
"When you're dead I'll be able to do what I want! I can't
wait!" Francie had replied.'**

But now Francie's mum *is* dead, and all Francie can remember are
their arguments and her angry words. She feels totally lost, not
knowing how she's supposed to feel and wishing she hadn't been
so cruel. Then Francie discovers her father crying in the kitchen,
and he yells at her to leave him alone. Francie's really hurt and
confused. What *do* people expect of her?

'**Coherent and powerful.**' *Times Literary Supplement*

Fiction £3.99
ISBN 0 7043 4947 7

Sandra Chick
Push Me, Pull Me

**Winner of the Other Award and shortlisted for the
Observer Teenage Fiction Prize**

**'This man from nowhere just walks in, takes my mother
from me, takes me from myself . . .'**

Cathy has a problem: her mother's new boyfriend, Bob. He's
moved in, taken over their lives and all her mum seems to care
about these days is keeping him happy. Then, one day, Cathy's
world really falls apart. Bob rapes her. And no amount of washing
can take away the pain or the guilt. Until slowly, her anger
surfaces and she begins to work it out . . .

Fiction £2.95
ISBN 0 7043 4901 9

Alison Hadley of Brook Advisory Centres, editor
Tough Choices
Young Women Talk About Pregnancy

Recommended by Brook Advisory Centres

'I had a gut feeling that I was pregnant. I confided in my best friend and we decided to get a pregnancy test after school. I was so scared waiting for the result. The two blue lines confirmed my worst nightmare – I was pregnant.'

What would you do if you found yourself pregnant unexpectedly? Would you keep the baby, put it up for adoption or opt for a termination? And what about parents, friends, school? Could you rely on your best friend to keep a secret? Where would you turn for help and advice? What would life be like with a new baby? In this moving and powerful collection, young women share the difficult choices they've made, and reflect on how their pregnancy affected their lives – from dealing with the emotional consequences of a termination, to the joys and tribulations of being a young mother. A riveting, thought-provoking and compelling read, *Tough Choices* gives a powerful insight into teenage pregnancy.

Non-fiction £4.99
ISBN: 0 7043 4953 1

grab a livewire!
save ~~£££s~~!!! with this voucher

Buy any of the following books and get
£1 off each book you buy! Post-free!

save £££s with this voucher!

On the Rocks by Sandra Chick

Cheap Street by Sandra Chick

I Never Told Her I Loved Her by Sandra Chick

Push Me, Pull Me by Sandra Chick

Tough Choices edited by Alison Hadley of
Brook Advisory Centres

Name _____

Address _____

_____

_____

Postcode _____

I would like:

_____ copies of **On the Rocks** at £3.99 less £1 = £2.99

_____ copies of **Cheap Street** at £4.99 less £1 = £3.99

_____ copies of **I Never Told Her I Loved Her** at £3.99 less £1 = £2.99

_____ copies of **Push Me, Pull Me** at £2.95 less £1 = £1.95

_____ copies of **Tough Choices** at £4.99 less £1 = £3.99
(NB. **Tough Choices** is available from September 1999)

_____ Livewire catalogue

Total enclosed £ _____

Do not send cash through the post. Send postal orders (from the Post Office)
in pounds sterling or cheques made out to The Women's Press.

Send this form and your cheque or postal order to The Women's Press,
34 Great Sutton Street, London EC1V 0LQ Allow up to 28 days for delivery.
Do remember to fill in your name and address!

This offer applies only in the UK to the books listed above, subject to availability.
This voucher cannot be exchanged for cash. Cash value 0.0001p